Paco:
A Collection of
Short Stories

T.M. Jacobs

Also by T. M. Jacobs

Non-Fiction

*Goodspeed's Folly: The Life of William Henry Goodspeed
and his Opera House*

*Basic Tips & Information on
Research, Writing & Self-Publishing*

*Milestones & Memories: The History of
St. George Parish Community Church*

*H. E. Heitman: An Early Entrepreneur
of Fort Myers, Florida*

*The 1864 Diary of Union Civil War Soldier
Sergeant Samuel E. Grosvenor (2nd Edition)*

*Peek Into The Past: A Collection of
Lee County Historical Articles - Vol. I & II*

The Little Book of Writing Advice

Fiction

*Necropolis Knights: The Gravetime Society
of Seven Cemetery*

The Little Black Book of SINS

Ava, I'm Sorry

Poetry
The Seeding of a Rose

Movie Script
After The Heist

Dedication

This collection is dedicated to two gentlemen who have greatly impacted my writing. My high school English teachers:

William "Bill" Alberino, who taught me no matter what happens in life, I always have my writing which can and does serve as a process to keep me grounded.

The late Frank Barron, who taught me there is a story everywhere, just open your eyes.

Thank you Mr. A. Lunch after COVID-19?

Thank you Mr. B. Your words and wisdom are greatly missed.

Introduction

For years, I've wanted to compile a collection of short stories. The only challenge: I stopped writing short stories about twenty-five years ago. I began to focus more on my non-fiction writing, and most of the short stories I had written disappeared with the ever-changing world of technology.

Then, the inspiration to write short stories again hit me. I started to churn out a short story once a week. While some were no good and will remain in a much less opened folder on my computer, some had a bit of merit to them.

From 2016 to 2018, I shared some of these with various writing groups and entered others in contests. The themes vary from horror (*Ghost Music*) to Twilight Zone-ish (*The Sound of White Noise*) to a nostalgic tale (*My Penance: The Diary of the Old Leatherman*). A few were born from the game Storymatic, where participants pull a couple of cards and use them as writing prompts.

My goal with this collection is for you to enjoy reading these stories as much as I did writing them!

T.M. Jacobs
(2020 upstate NY)

Second Thought

Introduction: The seed for this short story was planted in my mind while in high school. In Literary Composition Class, we reviewed a story (I cannot recall the title) in which the main character climbed out onto a ledge to retrieve a piece of paper. I immediately began to write (in my head) a story of a character climbing out onto a ledge. Years later, I wrote this short story, which has been well received by numerous writing groups.

Thirty-year-old Morgan Dean placed his favorite pen on his desk. He tore the single sheet of crisp white paper from the pad and began to read his words, admiring his penmanship.

"Are you still with me, Morgan?" a voice on the other end of the phone asked.

He put the paper down. "Yeah, I'm still here."

"I think you made a good decision, a great one, in fact. You know you can call anytime if you need to. Someone is always here, and I'm glad you had a second thought."

"Me too," Morgan spoke softly.

"Again, I'm glad you called. Have a good day."

"You too."

Just as the phone call ended, a gust of wind blew through the open window of Morgan's living room in his five-story high-rise apartment, and the paper flew out the open window.

"No!" Morgan dropped his cell phone and ran to the window leaning out as far as possible. He jerked his head in a few directions, then saw the paper stuck to an uninhabited bird's nest on the narrow ledge. "Great," he muttered.

He paced in his apartment for a few minutes, continually checking to make sure the paper had not been swept away. He sat on his leather couch, ran his fingers through his hair and over his heavy five o'clock shadow. "I need that paper," he said aloud. "God knows what people would think if they read it. I've got to get that paper."

A couple of minutes later, a thought struck him. He removed his shoes and socks and hurried back to the open window. Then he carefully climbed out onto the eighteen-inch ledge facing the building and slowly shuffled his way toward the nest.

No one below or even across the way had noticed Morgan shuffling along the ledge five stories above the ground. From the corner of his eye, he could see his neat hand-writing on the piece of paper that fluttered and began to tear as the wind picked up.

Just a few more feet, he thought. "I can do this," he said. "I just can't look down. Don't look down."

Morgan carefully slid his left foot sideways, then his right. "Just a little more...." He paused to let his heartbeat catch up and rebuild a bit of courage to continue. Then, he heard a faint voice from the street below. "Oh my god! He's gonna jump!"

"No, I'm not," he said, although no one could hear him. "I'm not jumping. Not today, not now, not ever." A couple of minutes later, he knew that a crowd had gathered on 67th Avenue. He imagined that people were pointing, whispering, shouting—and some might have been praying—but he would not, could not, look down. He started to lose his breath and began to panic. *Breathe. Breathe in, breathe out.*

The paper again fluttered as a gust of wind, the strongest yet, blew across the side of the building. Morgan inched a little closer to the paper and closed his eyes for a moment. Turning his head, he opened his eyes only to be staring into the direct bright sunlight. He squinted, trying to focus on the nest.

As he drew in a breath and bent down to retrieve the paper, a booming voice came over a bullhorn. "Please make your way back to the open window! You don't want to do this!" Again, Morgan tried not to look down. "I'm Sergeant Ted Moore with the city police!" the voice continued. "I'm here to help you!"

Morgan straightened up, leaned forward against the brick building, and began to breathe in quick short huffs. "I'm not going to jump," he said to no one. "I just want to get my paper back."

***

Eric Hunt returned home from work at 5:30 p.m. to find his wife, Sara, glued to her laptop in the kitchen. "Whatcha watch'n?" he asked, coming up behind her and kissing her neck.

"Some guy is out on the ledge down on 67th Ave."

"That's sad."

"You don't like seeing these kinds of things, I know."

"Well, spending hours operating a suicide helpline, listening to people who feel they have nothing to live for, then to come home to this. . . It's depressing. Now what's going through my mind is why didn't this guy call us. If only I could have talked to him, who knows. Maybe he'd be doing anything but standing out on a ledge."

"You can't save everyone."

"I know, but I'd like to think I can save at least one life, at least his."

Eric's wife shut down her laptop and gave him a long, needed hug. "How about an early dinner out tonight? My treat?"

"Sure."

Thirty minutes later, Eric and Sara, hailed a cab

and headed to Thistle Key Grill, where they had met just last year. Eric had been out with his friends for happy hour while Sara waited for a blind date who never showed. They clicked and were now enjoying the delights of matrimony.

***

Morgan carefully crouched down and extended his now shaking hand and arm out toward the nest, as he inched closer. The sun beating down caused sweat to form across his forehead, rolling down into his eyes, stinging them. He slowly straightened back up and wiped his eyes the best he could.

"Please make your way back to the open window," Sgt. Moore ordered.

"I've got to get that paper," Morgan whispered. "I've had a second thought and can't let anyone read it."

Steadying himself, he crouched further down and took in a deep breath. His fingertips were barely touching the paper when the wind blew, causing it to curl just out of his reach "God damn this wind!" he said under his breath.

With one final reach, Morgan snatched the paper between his index and forefinger. "Got it!"

He stood up, clutching the paper in his hand … and then looked down. The world below him began to spiral. He now heard the sirens, the shouts of the onlookers, and even the helicopter circling above. Nausea wreaked havoc in his stomach. Sweat poured out of every pore in his body.

***

Eric and Sara finished their meal and hailed a cab.

"Where ya headed?" the driver asked.

"To 45th West and Broad Street," Eric replied.

"Can't go that way. I'll have to take you around to get to 45th."

"Why?"

"They got it sectioned off. Some nut out on a ledge."

"Oh my God! He's still up there?" Sara asked.

"Well, whichever way you need to go, please do so," Eric said, slipping his hand into Sara's and squeezing it.

***

Morgan's arms swirled as his knees buckled. He tried to grab onto the bricks, but one foot slipped. He did one last turn and fell face-first from the ledge, still clutching the paper in his hand.

The crowd let out a massive gasp as he plummeted to the ground. A loud thud echoed along the street when Morgan's body hit the asphalt. Reporters began taking photos as the police tried to control the crowd. An ambulance backed up to where his body lay. Morgan's second thought had cost him his life.

A policeman gently pried the paper from Morgan's hand and read the note.

Dear Sara,

My life is upside down. I should have shown up. I should have gone to Thistle Key Grill, yet I took the path of being scared and afraid to embrace what the future may have had in store. That cowardly action of not showing up changed my life because I've done nothing but miss you since. We exchanged emails and spent hours on the phone. Although we never met, we somehow fell in love. I felt like you rescued me from the life I was living. You made me smile, but then you stopped taking my calls or answering my texts or emails. I can't rightfully blame you, for it was me who didn't show. And now I have no more tears. This note is my solution to end the pain.

Miss you, Sara, my Angel.

M. Dean

***

Eric and Sara watched the news as the anchor informed viewers of how Morgan Dean jumped off the ledge in an apparent suicide. According to the letter, the anchor said he was heartbroken over someone he felt he loved yet never got to meet.

Eric and Sara looked at one another. "Is that the Morgan you told me about when we first met?" Eric asked. "The guy who didn't show up?"

"I-it ... must be," she whispered as tears filled her eyes.

"Wow. I spoke with him this morning. He said he had had a second thought." Eric paused to dab her eyes with the cuff of his shirt. "I guess you couldn't rescue him, and I couldn't save him."

Without saying another word, they held each other tight.

Memories to Ashes

Introduction: This short-short story came about from a picture writing prompt contest (700-word limit) by Writer's Digest. The photo is below.

Henry Hoffman stood at the water's edge, bowing his head in a silent prayer for Emilia, his wife of fifty-four years. This would be Henry's final good-bye to his bride, his companion, and best friend. When they immigrated from Germany in 1944, before the war was officially over, they promised always to walk the beach hand in hand. Now, Henry had no hand to hold, only memories to cherish.

The city was their home, but the beach became their sanctuary. Emilia would often share with him how she believed we all came back. "We do," she told him once. "We come back to see and feel our loved ones. I will come back to you, Henry. My love for you is unending."

The final stages of emphysema set in two days later, stealing her last breath without a word. Her hand went limp in Henry's, and he knew, at last, she had found peace.

The battle against this disease didn't stir Henry. The four years of Emilia's Alzheimer's, however, rocked him to his core. As her memory faded, they no longer shared conversations revisiting the day they met, or the day they fell in love, or the day he proposed at the beach by having a heart drawn in the sand with, "Will you marry me?" etched in it. But the worst was the day she no longer recognized him. That's when Henry's heart shattered. He felt his world, their world, slip away.

Following her wishes, Henry brought her to the beach one last time. This visit, perhaps more for him than her, would be his last. Although his pace had slowed over the years, he walked with her along the shore, breathing in the salt air, watching the seagulls take flight, and letting his feet get wet as the water kissed the shore. He mumbled a few words in his native German tongue, twisted the lid off the urn, and sprinkled her ashes into the sea. "Come back to me, Emilia," he whispered through his tears. "Please, come back."

Henry stood still with his pant legs rolled up, tipping his hat, missing her. Just by looking out at the vast ocean, he could hear her voice, and as the warm water ran up to his feet and they sunk into the sand, he knew it was her way of touching him.

It only took a minute before Emilia's ashes were gone, swallowed by the water, which served as her place of happiness. This place had been where she said "yes" to the man of her dreams, and where she told Henry after two years of marriage, they were to become a family. Now she had become one with the earth, while her soul, Henry hoped, stayed beside him.

As he turned around and began his first walk without her hand, he heard a soft voice. Carried by the wind, it came right to his ear. "I'm here, Henry. I'm here."

***

Henry awoke to his nurse, gently shaking him. "It's time for your medicine, Mr. Hoffman. Please sit up."

"Why do you do that?" he grunted in a huff.

"Do what?"

"Wake me up every time she's almost back with me?"

"We've been through this before, Mr. Hoffman. Please,

take your medicine, then you can rest some more."

Henry swallowed his pills from the cup his nurse handed him, followed by a glass of water, then the nurse left his room. Laying back on his bed, he reached over to the nightstand and grabbed a little bottle filled with a mixture of sand and ash. He clutched it to his chest and closed his eyes, as his words filled the air: "Please come back to me, Emilia. Please, come back."

The Sound of White Noise

Introduction: This short story was first published in Katatim Short Horror Stories Vol. 1 (2017). *I had worked with the story's outline and thought of expanding it into a novel, but feel it works better as a short story. It appears in a more extended version here than what was published in* Katatim.

The airplane rattled across the open sky. The only comparison I could think of was being on an old wooden roller coaster where you're slammed side to side, praying it doesn't fall apart. Before you have time to readjust your body or brace yourself, you're smashed up against the other side of the cart, and holding onto the rail in front of you does little to no good.

This jump was to be our last to complete our training. The two and a half weeks were rough but went by fast. I caught one more glance out the open side and could see a massive cloud formation below.

"Check all your lines, make sure you're connected to the runner," a large, black man hollered. "We don't want to lose anyone on the last jump."

"Are you ready for this?" Michael Simmons asked. He had signed up for three years and was on his last month.

"Ready as I'll ever be," I replied.

"When we land, I'll buy the first round."

"Sounds good to me. I could use one. I'm not a big fan of jumping out of perfectly good airplanes."

"Well, I wouldn't call this perfectly good, so double-check your lines," he said. "We had a fella last month who didn't, and it wasn't a pretty sight when we found him."

I tugged on my lines and rechecked my connections.

"Line up, gentlemen!" the black guy ordered. "On the count of three, you jump. No hesitations, no second thoughts, you jump! If you want to say a prayer, say it on the way down."

Along with thirteen other men, Michael and I lined up single-file and jumped out the side of the plane one by one. As I neared the edged, I drew in a deep breath, said a quick prayer, then stepped out into nothing. The wind was harsh against my face. My ears were ringing as if I had just left a loud rock concert, and my eyes were watering. I was now free-falling at 14,000 feet. That's when my connection line engaged, pulled me back up, and my chute opened.

I can't say that for the guy who shot past me

screaming for his mother. "Pull the ripcord," I hollered, only to have my instructions disappear into the wind as he raced toward what would surely be his demise. Looking left and right, I took note of about nine other chutes from our group. I was right above Michael as he and I descended into a heavy fog. Then I lost sight of him and the others. Oddly, it felt as if the fog was slowing my fall. The wind wasn't as strong, my eyes no longer were watering, and the ringing in my ears disappeared.

I felt like I was suspended in the fog for a fair amount of time; when I checked my watch, it had stopped. Stopped at the exact moment I jumped. The air felt eerie ... something was changing. The temperature, air quality, and density seemed different. This was unlike any other jump, and the fog was sticking to me.

As I peered into the gray fog, an old saying came to mind: "The fog's so thick that I can't see my hand in front of my face." There was even an odd taste. Actually, that's what was weird; the fog had a taste to it. It wasn't like smoke or dry ice after being submerged in water, and it wasn't a misty taste either. This fog was different from what I've experienced mountain climbing or being in a harbor early in the morning.

Besides my watch, my two-way radio didn't work, and my compass needle was spinning counter-clockwise. "What the hell?" I mumbled.

The fog finally broke, and the ground below grew closer. Not far from where I would land, I saw another chute on the ground. I braced myself for contact, keeping my knees slightly bent. The landing was soft, and the chute spread about the area seconds after I hit the ground. *Where am I?* I wondered. Nothing looked familiar. I released the chute from my waist and walked over to the chute I had seen. It was number 0706. "Michael's," I said aloud. "Michael!" I hollered. "It's time for that beer you promised me." No answer. "Come on, Michael. You know how I hate your stupid games. Come on out!" *Damn guy, probably at the tavern without me.*

I looked around his chute and tried to track the direction he may have gone, but it was useless. It seems that we landed in a vast empty field, with no grass. This meadow or prairie was not like the ones back home. It had no mountains in the distance, not a river or stream nearby, and no trees anywhere, just an odd sand texture. It was like a desert without the heat and sand.

Looking at the sun's position, I knew there were only a few hours of daylight left. Michael left no tracks, which was perplexing. I turned around and looked at the ground. I left no footprints either. *What the hell is this place?* The sun rises in the east and sets in the west; if that's true here, I decided to head toward the sun, due west.

After two hours, something caught me off guard. *Why did I not have an appetite or feel the need to quench my thirst?* Rummaging through my backpack, I pulled out some nuts and dried fruit. Putting a small handful into my mouth, I immediately spat it out. The snack didn't have a stale taste, but more like a sharp sour bite to it. I checked the date on the package, and they were still suitable for another two weeks.

"Michael!" I hollered again. Silence, followed by a distant howling sound. "Is anybody here?" I yelled. The howling grew a bit louder. A few seconds later, a massive storm came barreling at me. With no way to protect myself, I laid on my stomach, putting my backpack over my head and pulled it down over my ears. I shut my eyes tight and held onto the back pack as if my life depended on it. The wind was fierce as if I were still free-falling from the plane. It felt like a sandblaster against my backside as the grains of dirt swirled about my body. Ten seconds later, it was gone—entirely.

I got up and looked at the sun again, this time realizing it was not like the sun back home. I did not need to squint, and there was no burning sensation in my eyes from staring into the orange orb. Even as the sun prepared to set, there seemed to be no change in temperature.

Just before the sun was to disappear behind the blurry horizon, which appeared to be the edge of this desolate tract of land, it switched directions and began to rise again. I stopped and watched in disbelief. *What the heck?* So much for following the "sun sets in the west."

I continued walking in the same direction, hollering for Michael a few more times, with no answer, then I noticed a house about one hundred yards in the distance.

As I got closer, I could see it was in dire need of a coat of paint; the wood clad siding was weather beaten. The window shades were drawn, and the house showed no signs of being lived in. The front yard was dirt, no grass. There were no flowers, no shrubs, no walkway, no stonewall, no fence, merely a yard looking like a desert. As they would say in real estate, the place had zero curb appeal. I rapped on the door, and a few moments later an older man wearing blue jeans, black shoes, and a white-collar shirt cracked it open.

"Can I help you with something?" he asked in a scratchy voice.

"Yes. Exactly, where am I?"

"You're in Townland," he said with a smile.

"Townland? I'm afraid I never heard of it."

"Well, it's here. Would you like to come in for a cup of coffee?"

"That would be great if it's no trouble." Even though I still had no thirst, I was hoping this gentleman could explain where I was and hopefully find Michael.

"If it were trouble, I wouldn't have thrown out the invite."

As he opened the door and stepped back, I crossed the threshold and immediately noticed the walls were unpainted sheetrock, completely bare. There was no furniture other than a table and two chairs. The floors had no hardwood flooring, tile, or carpet, only plywood.

"Just moved in?"

"Nope. Been here twenty years now."

"Twenty years?"

"Yes. Why ya so surprised?"

"Not to be rude, but twenty years and you haven't painted or hung a picture?"

He looked at me, perplexed as if I spoke in a foreign tongue. "Not sure I follow. What do you mean by 'painted or hung a picture'?"

"Why haven't you decorated in all the years you've been here?"

"Decorated?" He shook his head.

"This looks like a beautiful home. Why not spruce it up? Hang some wallpaper or artwork?"

I then realized he also had no books or a bookshelf; there was no TV, no stereo, no knick-knacks, or even a rug. I had a clear view to the back of the house, and looking out the sliding glass door I could tell his neighbor's house was identical.

"Grab a chair," he motioned. "I'll get the coffee."

As he turned to head toward the kitchen, his steps were slow, purposeful. Each time he lifted and placed his foot back down, it was like magnets were pulling his feet back down.

"Are you all right, sir?" I asked.

"Why sure. And the name's Sam."

"It just looked like you might have a bit of difficultly walking."

"No. I walk just fine. Never felt better in all my days."

I still couldn't get over twenty years, and his place was empty. *How does anyone live like this? Surely insanity can't be far behind for him. Maybe I'd be better off getting into town and search for Michael there.* "I think I will pass on the coffee. Thank you, anyhow."

"Suit yourself."

"How far into town? And could you possibly tell me where the local tavern is?"

"About five miles due west is the center of town."

"Thank you again."

He slowly made his way to the front door and watched me leave.

The sun was still rising, although from the west instead of the east. Still no change in temperature either, and I feared another storm could come at any time.

Three hours into my walk, I checked my compass, and it was pointing east, yet I knew I was heading west. *Maybe I got the sun's direction wrong? What if I was heading east when I thought I was heading west? Maybe this place is the polar opposite of home?* Regardless, I continued to walk in the same direction, leaving no footprints.

As I got closer to the town, it was hard not to notice all the houses were exact duplicates like they were constructed with a cookie cutter, and not one was painted. Same for all the other buildings. *How do they tell these apart?*

Within what seemed like an hour, I arrived in town. I entered the Townland Tavern and sat at the bar. Oddly there was no jukebox, no pictures, no TVs hanging on the walls, no color or decorations whatsoever. Then it dawned on me, *I never passed a library in town, no bookstore, or movie theater, there wasn't even a car dealership.*

"Here you go," the bartender said, placing an icy cold beer in front of me.

"How did you know I wanted a beer?"

"What else would you be wanting?"

"It just that I didn't order a beer, so I'm puzzled that you knew I was going to ask for one. Are you psychic?"

"Am I what?" hollered the bartender. "What the hell is a psychic?"

"Never mind," I said, grabbing the beer and taking a gulp. "By any chance, did you see a man come in here, dressed like me, goes by the name Michael?"

"Michael? What the heck is a Michael?"

"Michael isn't a what; it's a who. You've never heard the name Michael?"

"Can't say I have."

The bells above the door jingled and two men dressed identically, as if they were twins, walked in.

"Hi Sam," they both said.

"Good day, Sam. How about a beer?" the bartender said. "And how about you, Sam? Ready for a cold one?"

Did I hear this conversation correctly? Are they all named Sam? Then I realized the bartender was also dressed like them—blue jeans, a white-collar shirt, and black shoes. "Excuse me?" I asked. "You are all named Sam?"

"What else would we be named?" The three men laughed. "Why? What be your name?"

"I'm Mark."

"Mark?" one of the gentlemen questioned. "Why are you named Mark? A mark is a spot, not a name."

"Before you got here, he was going on about someone named Michael."

"Michael?" the other Sam questioned. "That's a strange name."

"I don't understand. Everyone is dressed the same, has the same name. You have no music, no books, what the hell is this place?"

"What are books?"

"Yeah. What exactly is music?"

I furrowed my brow. "How do you live like this? How do you live where everything and everyone is the same?"

"What's wrong with Sam being the same as me?"

"Yeah," chimed in the bartender, giving me the eye. "What's wrong with Sam being the same as me?"

"Same as me," I mumbled. "Same. As. Me. Good Lord, where the hell am I?"

I walked out into the street and hollered for Michael. I scanned up ahead and saw him turn a corner. I ran and caught up to him before he disappeared into a house. "Michael," I said, grabbing him by his shoulder, spinning him around. "I'm so glad to see you. Where the hell are we?"

"We are in Townland, and I'm not Michael. I'm Sam. And you are the same as me."

"No. No. You're Michael. Michael Simmons. We just parachuted down here. You must have gone through the fog as I did."

Michael stared at me in disbelief as I did to him. Then I shook my head and quick-stepped back to the Townland Tavern. "Can you explain what you mean by 'the same'?" I asked one of the Sam's, after I stepped inside. "Why is nothing or no one different?"

All three replied in unison: "Different?" Then they looked at me, puzzled.

I blew out a deep breath, then walked back out into the street, feeling almost dazed when it hit me: even the trees, the birds, and the clouds were all the same. Same size, height, and I'm willing to bet the trees had the same number of leaves too.

"Where the hell am I?" I screamed, falling to my knees. "What's happening to me? Why is everything the same? Somebody, please! God, help me!"

An older man, who I'm sure was named Sam, came up to me. "I'm not sure who God is, but you're in Townland. The place with no imagination."

Just then, people came out of their houses, all dressed the same. Women had the same hairdos, the men neatly shaved, children all looking like mirror reflections. They gathered in the street and circled me, chanting, "Townland, no imagination. Townland, no imagination," over and over. They moved in closer and closer. I put my hands over my ears, trying to drown out their words. Looking up to the sky, I saw nothing but a vast blue canvas. I closed my eyes and screamed.

It was at that moment, my memory cleared. I could no longer remember any songs or bands, and couldn't recall any books I had read. I no longer knew different colors, artwork, or TV programs. Everything from my childhood, my yesteryears, was gone from my memory. *How am I supposed to live now, in a world devoid of imagination?*

In my mind, no answer came. All I could hear was the sound of white noise in an empty vacuum.

"Townland, no imagination," I whispered.

Woodstock Baby

Introduction: This story came about from playing Storymatic. The words were Guest, Former Child Star, *and* Overly Large Gift.

The audience gave a round of thunderous applause when Ted Shores announced the next guest to appear on his "Talk with Ted from the Shores Show." It was none other than former child star, Billy Bunting.

At age ten, Billy starred in *Driving Me Crazy*, a sitcom that ran from 1960-65. Things didn't go smoothly for him after the show got canceled. He became fond of the bottle at age fifteen, leading to a string of runs-in with the police. By 1969, at the age of nineteen, he had already been through rehab twice.

When he walked out on the stage, he was now fifty years old, bald, a bit on the husky side, and wearing coke bottle eyeglasses. He waved at the enthusiastic crowd and sat next to Ted.

"Welcome to the show Billy."

"Thanks. It's great to be here."

"I'm just going to jump right in, Billy. We have something for you. Are you ready?"

"I've seen your show, and I'm as ready as I'll ever be."

Ted turned to face the crowd. "Audience, are you ready?"

They responded with a hearty, *"Yes, Ted!"*

"Well, alright, then. Please roll it out."

Two stagehands rolled out a huge box and placed it in front of Billy.

"What is it?" he asked.

"Well, let's have a look, shall we?" With that, Ted opened the box, and a thirty-year-old man stepped out.

"Hi, Dad!" he said to Billy.

"Hi ... *Dad?*" Billy questioned.

"That's right," Ted said. "Back in 1969, while at Woodstock, you got a bit lucky with a young girl named Susan Trappons. Well, she's been looking for you. Susan, come on out."

"I don't' believe this," Billy mumbled. Then he looked at the audience. "I'm sorry to disappoint you all, but I was never at Woodstock. I don't know Susan, and I'm not the father."

"Oh, come on, Dad," the thirty-year-old said.

"Don't call me that."

"Audience," Ted said, "do they look like father and son?"

The audience let out a loud, *"Yes, Ted!"*

"No! No way!"

"Hi, Billy. Why do you deny this?" Susan asked while taking a seat beside Billy.

"There's nothing to deny. I'm not the father. I wasn't at Woodstock. This is absurd."

Ted turned to Susan. "Talk to us. Tell Ted from the Shores what happened."

Susan adjusted in her chair and brushed her blonde bangs away from her eye. "Well, I can prove Billy is the father of Hunter. I remember Woodstock, and I can even describe Billy's nether region."

"Ohhh," groaned the audience.

"Whoa, whoa," Ted said with a low pitch in his voice. "We're going there, are we?"

Susan smiled. "For starters, I can tell you he's not large—"

"Ohhh," the audience groaned again.

"Wait, wait. He's also not below average either," she said with a grin.

Billy hung his head down and ran his hands through his hair and over his face when he noticed camera three came in for a close-up. "This is ridiculous."

"Anything else?" Ted asked.

"As a matter of fact, yes. Believe it or not, Billy has a real cute mole shaped like a pear."

"You don't say," Ted smiled and gave a glance toward Billy.

"And..." Susan continued. "It's right on the head of his..." She blushed. "I can't say it."

"Oh, go on. We're all adults here. Isn't that right audience?"

"Yes, Ted," they said in unison.

"Well, he calls it his—"

"Look!" Billy shouted. "This has gone far enough. Again, I was not at Woodstock, and I've never met Susan."

"He calls it his Love Dart, and he always tries to hit the bullseye," Susan giggled and the audience roared.

"Well, there's certainly one way we can settle this,"

Ted said, looking straight into the camera. "Billy, drop your pants and show us what you got."

"What? Are you freak'n crazy? I'm not going to drop my pants on national TV. This is insane."

Ted turned to face the studio audience and, with a broad smile, said, "Audience, what do ya think?"

"Drop your pants, drop your pants," they chanted.

"Ah, come on, Dad. Just take one for the team."

"Team? What the hell, we are not a team! There is no team! This is ridiculous! I'm outta here."

"Now, Billy," Ted said. "That's not the way to behave when you've just been reunited with your son."

A vein on Billy's neck began to pulse, his eyes squinted, and he drew in a large breath. Then he stood up and walked off the stage. Back in the green room, he slammed the door and demanded to be left alone.

Ted stood up and asked for the audience to quiet down. "I'm going to see if I can't get Billy to come back out and join us." He then signaled for a cameraman to follow him. He walked down a corridor and knocked on a door that had a sign that read "Greenroom."

"Billy? We'd like for you to rejoin us out on stage. I have DNA results, so why don't you come back, and we'll let the DNA determine if you're the father or not? We all know, DNA doesn't lie."

The Greenroom door creaked open a bit. Billy peered out and saw Ted with his huge smile of white pearlies and perfectly groomed brown hairpiece. Ted stepped through the doorway and put his arm around Billy. "Come on," he said, the audience is waiting.

There was an uproar of applause as Billy came back onto the stage. He moved his chair away from Susan and her son and sat down. "Audience," Ted said. "What do I hold in my hand?"

"DNA results!" the audience replied and cheered.

"And what do we know about DNA?"

"DNA never lies!"

"That's right!" Ted looked over at Billy, then to Susan and Hunter. "Are we ready?"

All three nodded.

Ted tore through the envelope with his forefinger, blew into it, and pulled out a yellow piece of paper. As he unfolded it, the audience grew quiet. The cameras zoomed in for close-ups on all three guests. "According to the DNA results ... Billy ... you are *not* the father of Hunter."

The audience went crazy, screaming, and gasping. Billy stood and gave a mighty fist pump into the air, followed with an, "I told you so!"

Susan and Hunter looked at each other in disbelief.

Ted stood up and quieted the audience. "Now, Billy, there's more."

"More?" Billy asked. "What do mean there's more? You just said DNA doesn't lie and that I'm not the father."

"Very true, very true," Ted said, still clutching the paper in his hand. "DNA doesn't lie. While you are not the father of Hunter, you are, however, his *brother.*"

"Bro!" Hunter exclaimed, jumping up and embracing Billy. "I always wanted an older brother!"

Billy shoved Hunter to the side, the audience went frantic, and Susan sat with her head hung down.

"Let me get this straight," Billy said. "Are you saying my father had an affair with *this* woman?" he pointed over to Susan.

"Billy, the results are conclusive. You and Hunter share the same genes and chromosomes from the same father."

Billy glanced over at Susan. "How do you know my father?"

"I ... I don't know him," Susan said, her face beginning to blush.

"DNA doesn't lie. Isn't that right, Ted?"

"I'm just as shocked as you." Ted turned to his studio audience. "Are you surprised by this outcome?"

"Yes, Ted!"

Billy stood up, looked at Ted, then over to Hunter and Susan. They both nodded at Billy. He then took off his wig, the coke bottle glasses, and peeled off a tight wax mask.

Ted's face grew long and his eyes bulged. "I don't believe it," he whispered, which the mic picked up.

"You've been had, Ted," said Evan Dixon with a wide smile. "Audience," said Evan. "Did Ted just fall hook, line, and sinker?"

"Yes, Evan!"

Ted stood up as Evan walked around the stage with his hands held up, savoring the victory of having pulled one over on Ted. "How the hell did you change the DNA results?"

"I didn't change them. This cat *is* my brother."

"And Susan?"

"She's our good friend. And may I say, a pretty damn good actress, too," Evan smiled at her.

Then, a sudden pain ripped through Evan's backside as Ted smashed a chair into him, knocking him to the floor. He pounced on Evan and beat him with an onslaught of punches. "How dare you humiliate me!"

Marcus Dixon, Evan's younger brother, who helped pull off this prank as Hunter Trappons, pried Ted off of Evan, along with two stage hands. The house lights flickered a few times, then came an announcement for the audience to please evacuate the studio as Ted was dragged backstage.

***

Evan dropped out of sight shortly after that stunt, which was dubbed the biggest prank on daytime talk TV. The world knew he would reappear sometime, somewhere, and pull off an even bigger prank, but as to where and when, nobody knew.

No charges were filed against Ted for the assault and his show was canceled not long after the incident.

With Ted out of a job and staying out of the public eye, and Evan nowhere on the radar, the only thing we're left with is: DNA doesn't lie, but sometimes people do.

Too Cold To Shed Any Tears

Introduction: This short story was also the result of a contest. Writer's Weekly conducts a quarterly writing contest where the entrants have 24-hours to write a story based on a theme emailed the day before. The theme for this particular contest: winter, extreme cold, and a girl wearing a scarf. My story received an honorable mention.

He never recalled it being this cold in all his years living in the country. Sure, it would rain, snow, and the temps would drop into the teens most nights, but this was different. Maybe it had to do with the moon and stars' alignment, perhaps an off-weather pattern like an El Nina hitting a warm pressure system. Either way, it didn't matter to Jonathan Markel.

Standing alone along the dirt road, which had frozen over, he shivered. Yet, he knew it was worth it as he rubbed his hands together, then put them back in his pockets. It had been too many years, and he needed to make amends.

Mandy Russell was barely going the speed limit because of her fear of black ice. Only two winters ago, she lost her father when he slid off the road into an embankment. Her life turned upside that evening when she received the news.

She was dressed in every winter garment she owned—snow pants, mittens, parka, and a scarf—because the heater in her old Pontiac didn't work. "I wish I could turn around," she mumbled. But she knew better and kept driving, cautiously.

As she rounded the bend, she saw him. There stood Jonathan, shivering, as he waved at her. When she pulled over, he quickly jumped into her car. "Good God, it's cold out. What took you so long?"

"The weather."

"Are you ready to do this?"

"Yes, I am. Are you?"

"I am. I just wished you picked a better day for it, that's all."

The snow-covered road stretched for miles. To either side, snowbanks blocked the view of the meadows. Jonathan drummed his fingers, while Mandy kept her focus on the road. This was not a stroll down memory lane; it was something they had to do.

"Why did you pick this day of all days?" Jonathan asked again.

"Because it's the anniversary of when dad died. Don't you remember? Oh, yeah, I forgot. Someone didn't bother to go to the funeral or even call mother," she snapped at him.

Jonathan ignored her abrasiveness and stared out the window. "Not sure why I need to be involved with all of this. Mother should have left everything to you."

"Because you need to sign the papers. Since you're forfeiting everything in the will to me, you need to be there in person, with the notary."

"Whatever," he mumbled as Mandy turned at the crossroads onto Pickerton Trail.

"You're going the wrong way, ya know."

"I'm pretty sure I know how to get there."

"I'm pretty sure ya don't."

An hour later, the road dead-ended at an old abandoned barn. Faded red with peeling white trim, holes in the roof, the barn stood stoic next to a silo leaning hard to the left.

"So, this is the place?" Jonathan questioned.

"Shut up," Mandy said as she climbed out of the car.

The wind picked up, and a flurry of snow began to fall. Jonathon rolled down the window and called out, "Let me guess. The notary and your lawyer are inside? Hope they got a nice roaring fire going. We're going to need it."

"I thought I told you to shut it?" Mandy looked about and shook her head. "Well, I guess we should head back."

She jumped back into the car and turned the key.

Click.

"You've got to be kidding me!" she said. She gave the key another crank.

Click.

"Oh, great," Jonathan groaned.

"Well."

"Well, what?"

"Get out and fix it, that's what."

"I'm no mechanic. Maybe you should have brought someone who knows their way around cars. Like your *husband*. Oh. Wait. I keep forgetting. He left you for someone saner."

Mandy got out of the car, slammed the door, and started walking toward the barn.

Jonathan got out and hollered, "You can't go in there, Mandy. You'll freeze to death. Your chances are better by staying in the car."

She turned back towards him and said something that was carried away by the gust of wind, then kept walking.

Jonathan got back in the car. Out of nowhere, a hawk swooped down, landing on the hood. It jerked its neck a couple of times, then took off toward a line of trees behind the barn.

Mandy thought of starting a fire but feared the whole barn would ignite. She took two horse blankets hanging in a stall to fight the cold and wrapped herself up in them. Still, the bite of Jack Frost kept nipping at her.

Slowly, the cold encased Jonathan and he fell into a deep sleep.

***

"*Son,*" said a voice. Jonathan opened his eyes and looked around.

"What? Who said that? Mandy?"

"*Son. It's me.*"

"What?" Jonathan said, seeing his breath.

"*You're going to be all right. Just wanted to tell you we're fine. Mother, Mandy, and I are fine, son. And you'll be all right.*"

"*No!*" Jonathan screamed. He bolted from the car and half ran, half stumbled toward the barn. He screamed a second time when he saw Mandy frozen in the blankets. He knelt beside her, but it was too cold to shed any tears.

Paco

Introduction: This short story came about through playing Storymatic. For this particular piece, the words were Laundry, Astronaut, *and* Slacker. *The beginning is what I came up with during the game; I've since added the middle and the ending.*

Today did not turn out as planned; it veered way off course, way out of my control. What should have been a day of coffee and reading, followed by dinner out, turned out into trouble that found me.

I walked into the Houston Wash 'n' Wear Laundromat around two in the afternoon. The sun was beating, and fighting a hangover made it no better. As I mentioned, I had other plans for today, but when someone vomits on your only set of clothes, well, plans change—instantly.

I traded a couple of dollars in for quarters.

"Here ya go," the kid behind the counter replied. He never glanced up from his phone during our transaction. In my mind, this kid would grow up to be a slacker; while most kids in Houston dream of becoming an astronaut, he seemed more preoccupied with texting.

As my clothes were spinning, I took a seat, wearing only my underwear and socks next to a haggard-looking man reading the newspaper. *Like, who reads newspapers nowadays?*

"Listen to me," he said in a scratchy voice. "We need to act fast."

"Um, act fast about what?"

"Follow my lead."

"Follow your—"

Before I could get another word out, he jumped up on the bench and pulled out a gun. "Everybody freeze, and I won't shoot. Paco," he said, throwing an empty laundry bag toward me. "Get their wallets, phones, jewelry."

"I'm not a part of this! And my name is not Pa–"

"Not now, Paco! Move! *Move!*" he said, waving his gun.

I didn't know what to do. I certainly didn't want to rob anyone. And I certainly didn't want to connect with any bullets.

A couple of customers sprinted out the door, leaving their laundry spinning into the next cycle. Other customers began to scream with a panic, while two ladies started to cry, begging for their lives.

"Wallets, gentlemen!" he shouted. "Ladies, let's empty those purses." He glanced over at me. "Come on, Paco. Open up those drawstrings and fill that bag up. This is ain't cowboy and Indians. It's the real thing!"

I tried to whisper to each customer as they put their belongings into the bag that I was not a part of this. That I was not Paco and apologized for what he was forcing me to do. When the last of the nine customers deposited his wallet and watch into the bag, the haggard man motioned for me to come to him.

"Let's get out here, Paco. Ya darn did good, amigo."

As I approached the bench he was standing on, I gave it a good shove, knocking him off balance. He fell face-first to the floor. Two guys reacted quickly; one jumped on him while the other retrieved the gun, which flew from his hand.

Immediately two loud bangs rang out. The haggard man no longer moved, and I felt a piercing sting in my right leg. As I unconsciously put my hand on my thigh, I could feel warm blood spilling out through my leg. My head began to spin, I became dizzy, and as I fell to the floor, the guy with the gun said, "Fuck you, Paco! I hope you die!"

Then everything went dark.

***

"So, let me get this straight. You went into the

laundromat," a uniformed police officer said as he scribbled on a small pad, "and sat next to this man who we now know as one Philip Shepard, whom you say you've never met before, but he was quick to include you in his robbery attempt? Is that what you want me to believe?"

"It's the truth," I said, in a hopefully convincing tone laced with a few moans. My heart monitor spiked up a bit, and my leg still had a pinched feeling. "I never met the guy. All I did was sit next to him while I was waiting for my laundry. Next thing I know, he jumps up on the bench, pulls out a gun, tosses me a bag, and tells me to rob everybody."

The officer looked over at his partner. "Sounds like a Quentin Tarantino film to me. How about you?"

"You said it."

"Look," the officer said as he flipped his pad closed and fixed his eyes back on me. "I spoke with the doctor, and you should be outta here by tomorrow. I suggest that you don't go too far. I might want to have another chat with you. Are we clear?"

"Yes," I answered in a huff. "Can hardly wait."

I laid back down, and as soon as the police left, my heart monitor relaxed. *How did I get into this situation?* I wondered. *All I wanted to do was a bit of laundry and then go about my business.*

***

I was discharged from the hospital two days following the surgery to remove the bullet from my leg. That morning, I left with my limp, and stopped at the pharmacy for my prescription. *Maybe there'll be another robbery in which I can play a part.* I tried to laugh at that thought, but I could barely raise a smile.

Once home, I propped myself up on the couch with my medicine, some water, a few snacks, and the remote.

Philip Shepard. Exactly who is this guy? Why did he pick me? Why did I happen to sit next to him?

I couldn't rest. Feeling anxious, I limped over to my small desk tucked into the corner of the living room. My laptop booted up, and I clicked over to the internet. Immediately I saw my mugshot followed by the headline: Two Robbers Get Cleaned-Up At Wash 'n' Wear.

Seriously? This is ridiculous. I'm not a robber. I'm an innocent bystander, for Pete's sake! And they used my mugshot. There are many great pics of me on my Facebook page and elsewhere in the social media world, and they choose my mugshot. Hell, even my driver's license photo would have been better.

The news article had even named me Myles "Paco" Anderson. Perhaps better than being called *Ma* like I was throughout high school, but *Paco?*

I got hotter under the collar as I read further. The article suggested toward the fact I was the one who had orchestrated the robbery—the botched robbery. *It wasn't botched. There was nothing to botch!* The reporter even dubbed us "Paco & Philly." *I don't even know this guy, and now the world thinks we're the next Bonnie and Clyde or Thelma and Louise. I guess this is my fifteen minutes of fame Andy Warhol mentioned back in 1968.* "In the future, everyone will be world-famous for 15 minutes," he said while in Sweden at one of his exhibitions. Well, this is undoubtedly not any fame I want.

The article went on to state how two good Samaritans saved the day. *What bullshit! I'm the one who risked my life when I slammed into the bench, knocking him down, which also got the gun out of his hand.*

Good Samaritan, my ass! The fucker shot me!

It turns out Philip Shepard died at the scene. Without questioning him for his side of the story or his motivation, the articles note that authorities feel I'm spinning a yarn a mile long.

Doing my search on Shepard, I found out that he was an economics professor at the state university for twenty-five years before disappearing two years ago. He left behind a wife and three teenagers. Funny how the article didn't mention any of this. They only portrayed him to be my partner in crime.

***

"I'm very pleased that you're willing to meet me," I said, with a slight crack in my voice.

"From what you told me over the phone, I felt it's the least I could do."

Her hand was warm, soft, and not a wrinkle to show. She still wore her wedding band and engagement ring. There was even a scent about her that she looked younger than her real age. "Like I said over the phone, Mrs. Shephard—"

"Please, call me Hannah," she said with a pleasant smile.

"Okay. Hannah. As I said, I'm not Paco and did not know, nor have I ever met your husband before that incident at the laundry mat. The media certainly has teamed us up as partners, but I was just at the wrong place at the wrong time."

"I believe you," she said in a hushed tone. "For me, it's like he died twice. I finally gave up on the idea that he would ever return, and now, well, he won't be returning."

"Mind if I ask what happened? How or why did he disappear?"

"I wish I knew," she said as she drew in a breath. "The last thing he said to me was he was going in search of Paco. And that was just over two years ago."

***

I learned that there were variations of a story, set in Spain, about a young boy named Paco who left home, and years later, his father went in search of him to tell his son all is forgiven. *Indeed, Philip must have known I was not his son, especially because we were too close in age. But what if he were drugged out? High in the sky? Who knows what he may have been thinking while at the laundromat?*

Hannah will now live the rest of her life without Philip, and I'll walk with a limp (sometimes painful, sometimes not) and the emotional scar of that afternoon for the rest of mine.

Eventually, all the media attention to this story faded. There were fewer and fewer articles, news reporters calling, TV stations looking for an interview, and people started to not recognize me as Paco or part of the duo who became known as the "Laundry Lunatics."

I moved to a new town some three hundred-forty miles away. I got a new job working at a golf pro shop, although my limp doesn't allow me to enjoy the sport. Even met a girl, Priscilla, who's sweet and never heard of the Paco story.

Today, I had a cup of coffee, did a little reading, and I'm sitting at home waiting for the delivery guy. I still get nervous around strangers, and I'm a bit on edge about this guy coming to my house, but I'm excited because he's delivering a washer and dryer.

My Penance:
The Diary of the
Old Leatherman

Introduction: This is based on The Leatherman, a figure clad in a make-shift suit of leather swatches who wandered in a 356-mile loop throughout New York and Connecticut from 1856-1889. Some of the news clippings are reprinted from the original source. It has long been a desire of mine to write a fictional account based on, "What if the Leatherman left behind a diary?" A factual article I wrote on him appeared in the Valley Courier newspaper back in 2001.

The Photograph

In the spring of 1900, Albert Dowd packed up the last of his gear, clutched his walking stick and set out from Mount Pleasant, New York, to follow in the footsteps of the old Leatherman. He was on a personal mission to learn all he could of the famed vagrant who wandered from town to town, never speaking, only begging for food, from the mid-1850s until he died in 1889.

Albert spent months preparing for his month-long trek. He was going to live this one month as if he were the Leatherman, sans the bulky patched leather suit. He traced his route and pinpointed where many of the caves and rock shelters were located through numerous accounts from the local papers. Unlike the Leatherman, Albert would have a compass, a lighter, and a small pistol for safety.

As he hiked through the small towns and villages, he struck up conversations with people who remembered the drifter. The tales were pretty much the same; he came through town, didn't talk much, avoided eye contact, gestured and grunted for some food, then continued on his way. Thirty-four days later, like clockwork, he'd return.

Every story's consequence was identical—no one knew his true identity, where he came from, or why he looped through New York and Connecticut.

On the twentieth day of his hike, Albert entered New Haven and met with John Rodders, a person who claimed to have personally known the Leatherman and even took a picture of him in 1884. They sat on Rodder's back porch and chatted over some iced tea.

"How is it you came to know the Leatherman?" Albert asked.

"First, tell me, tell me why on earth do you want to follow his trail? That's 365 miles according to most accounts."

Albert stirred his tea. "Well, I can't really explain what it is, but I feel some connection to him, and

I just want to learn as much as possible. And I'm almost finished with the loop. I've got about ten days to go."

"Fair enough." John took a sip of his tea, then sat back in his chair. "I met him in the summer of 1883. I gave him a hot meal, invited him to come inside, but he refused, as it was his custom never to set foot indoors. Exactly thirty-four days later, he came wandering through our town again. This time he let me take a photo of him, even removed his hat."

John handed Albert a photo of the Leatherman, holding a walking stick in one hand and a leather cap in the other. He wore a full beard and mustache, had tired eyes, and was so dirty people didn't know his race. "Did he talk at all? Say anything about where he came from or why he was wandering?"

"No. No, he never talked. He only gestured for some food, so I gave him half a loaf of bread, a jar of pickles, and some cheese. He wrapped everything into his sack and continued on his way."

Albert took a sip of his tea. "What about this deformity on his lip?" he asked, pointing to the picture. "I've read that he had throat cancer; is that true?"

"Yes. According to hospital records in Hartford, he was taken in by authorities to treat it, but somehow, he escaped and just continued with his walk. I believe his cancer got worse, then his lip got frostbite during the blizzard of 1888, and I feel that did him in."

"Sounds like a horrible way to go, if you ask me." Albert sipped his tea again, then put his glass down on the small wood table, and wiped his hand along his thigh to remove the wetness from the condensation forming on the glass. "If he was in so much pain, why wander from town to town? Or stay in one place, or even just end it all?"

John finished the last of his tea, then refilled his glass from the pitcher on the table. "That's the million-dollar question. No one knows why he did what he did. As others have, I can only speculate that his leather suit was worn to protect from the wind and rain. Leather does little, though, to keep out the cold. I'm not a hundred percent sold on the stories that the leather was worn as a reminder of something from his past."

"Do you know if anyone has claimed to have spoken to him? Eventually, I would think he would want a little bit of companionship."

"Hmmm ... Although he never did speak much, he did by chance write a note that he left with me." John reached down and picked up a leather-bound journal. Flipping through a few pages, he carefully pulled out a small piece of paper and pushed his eyeglasses up onto the bridge of his nose. "It reads, *Suivre mes pas, c'est connaitre mon ame,* which translates to, 'to follow in my footsteps is to know my soul.'"

John handed Albert the note. He looked it over a few times even though he knew no French. His penmanship was neat, as if he concentrated on each word when writing. "I guess that's what I'm doing," Albert said, handing the note back. "I'm tracing his steps to know his soul. I have hopes to discover who he truly was."

"Well, over the years, I've heard all about him but I can't say what was rightfully true and based on fact."

"Such as ..." Albert prodded.

"Well, one story is he was a criminal, on the run from the law. His leather outfit was nothing less than a disguise so the authorities wouldn't recognize him. Some say that's why he was constantly on the go and never stayed in one place too long." John took a long drink of his tea.

"What about you, do you believe that story?"

"No, actually, I don't. My feeling is life in prison would be preferable to the conditions Mother Nature lays out. For one thing, you have a bed and three meals a day. I, for one, wouldn't want to have been living outdoors when the blizzard of 1888 occurred."

"What do you think his reason was?"

"Hard to say. He may have had a broken heart, or maybe his marbles weren't going in the right direction. The truth is, I don't think we'll ever know. I believe his life will always be a mystery, and that's conceivably the way he wanted it."

Albert finished his tea and again glanced at the Leatherman's picture. "Too bad he never let anyone know his true identity."

"Right, and if wishes were horses," John said, picking up the two empty glasses. "I sincerely wish you the best on your journey, and may you find all the answers you're in search of, young man."

"Thanks so much for your time, sir. I do appreciate it."

"The pleasure was all mine," remarked John walking Albert to the front door, exchanging a handshake. "Here. This is now yours." John said, handing the photo to Albert.

"I can't take this, sir. Really. It's yours; you took it."

"Yes, indeed, and it is mine, which gives me the right to do with it as I see fit. I happen to see fit that this picture should belong to you. Maybe it will help you on your way. Some food-for-thought, sota-speak."

"Thank you, sir. Thank you very much. I'll be sure to be in touch if I find anything."

"Stay safe, young man. You still have a long ten-day hike ahead of you."

Albert continued on his way, now and then sneaking a glance at the picture of the Leatherman.

Discovering A Diary

Ten days later, Albert was coming full circle upon the last cave, the last stop for the Leatherman. The Dell Farm property had a narrow cave tucked into a small hillside. It was here, just a month ago, that Albert started his trek. It was also where, eleven years ago, two hunters who were tracking some deer found the Leatherman dead.

Peering into the cave, they noticed what they thought was a down-and-out person sleeping. Upon closer inspection, they realized it was the local legend—The Leatherman.

News of his death spread quickly among the small towns and villages dotted throughout Connecticut and along the Hudson River Valley in neighboring New York. Stories sprang up from all walks of life, stating they knew him, conversed with him, and knew why he was wandering all those years. Some stories were debunked immediately, while others faded with time.

Albert ducked his head and entered lying on his
back by shimming into the narrow shelter. Once
inside the cave, he sat down on the floor to drink
a half bottle of warm water, and he noticed a
squirrel busily digging and periodically chewing
on something. On closer inspection, he noticed the
squirrel was not chewing on an acorn, as one would
suspect, but what appeared to be a book. Shooing
the squirrel away, he gently dug around the edges
and discovered a leather-bound journal. It fit in the
palm of his hand.

He brushed the dirt off the surface and gave a
low whistle. "I can't believe I didn't find this last
month," he mumbled. *If this is what I think it is, my
prayers have been answered, and this whole month
of tracing his footsteps was well worth it.*

Albert opened the journal and carefully turned the
brittle pages. The penmanship was impeccable,
similar to the writing on the note John had given
him. Each stroke of the pencil accented the loops
and darkened the characters of the letters. It was
as if each word was carefully thought out before
being transferred onto the paper. He figured it
would take him a couple of hours, maybe longer, to
read through it.

*But who did he record this for? Was his plan to send
it back home eventually? And if so, to whom?*

The first page read:

Jonathan Laurent
Born Lyons, France, 1835
Mother Cadence Boivin
Father Pacifico Laurent

Une seule âme peut marcher sur la distance. (Only one soul can walk the distance.)

"It is!" Albert exclaimed out loud with no one to hear. *I can't believe it. It's his story. It's all about him.* He sat for a moment, awed that he was about to learn firsthand the Leatherman's true story. He turned the page and began to read.

19 March, 1889

It is with a shattered heart and a weak hand that I pen my tribulations. Call this my confession, call it my last testament, call it what you will. To me, it's the last time in which I'm allowed to reflect on my soul. My spirit died years ago; it seems likely it was a lifetime ago when it used to dance. My heart is now empty, with nothing left to give.

A light snowfall blanketed the farm last night. Temperatures not spring-like yet, but no wind or rain. I can feel God tugging at my soul, and soon I will proceed as my penance has been served. But before I depart, let me give you a sound understanding of who you refer to as "The Leatherman."

I didn't ask for this life, but I chose it.

I chose to don a suit of leather made from discarded patches weighing 60 lbs. Its mass would never compare to my burden. I carried my few worldly possessions in a hobo sack and chose to shelter in caves, make-shift huts, and sometimes in thick brush and under trees.

I came to this country a broken man, to serve a life penance which I imposed upon myself. After 30 years of trudging through the countryside, braving the winters, and battling the summers, my body has become worn, as a baseball mitt turned into soft hide after many ballgames.

My only desire in life was to be Catharine's husband and provide a stable, enriching, and loving environment. Our earnings came from her father, who brought me on as a partner in his leather business. Catharine made me a partner in her family. I not only failed the business and put her father into hardship, unable to pay his debts, but I also lost everything, including my reputation, status, and worst of all, Catharine's hand and heart.

I am not a criminal. Someone jilted in love and carrying the world's weight makes for a lost man, but not a criminal. And for these failures, I made a vow of silence and to wander endlessly, unlike any man before me.

May God bring me home to the light and let me sleep beside Him. This is my only prayer.

JL

The Old Leatherman's Diary
Part I

Let me say this: My atonement is to serve nothing more than to remind me of my failings. To exploit my shortcomings, to drive a stake into my soul.

I needed to come to America to escape the ridicule and demise of my inner being. My soul no longer sang, my heart lacked passion, and I was in pieces. And it is a tragedy of how this came to be.

In 1835, I was born to Pacifico Laurent and Cadence Boivin in Lyons, France. At the age of nine, I lost my father to the Franco-Moroccan war. He was an officer in the French fleet under the command of the Prince de Joinville. On August 14, 1844, when the Battle of Isly took place, he was shot in the back. The war ended a month later, with Morocco being victorious.

This put my mother and me into a new world—one of struggle and judgment. She took in laundry, and I left school at age ten to seek employment in the factory. I worked thirteen hours a day, and all of my sparse earnings went to mother.

Three years after losing father, mother was called to her eternal home of rest. I stayed on at the factory for two more years and boarded at a rundown institution for boys.

At fifteen, I left the factory and the boarding school. I spent the following five years traipsing around France, mostly in the city of Paris, sometimes getting into trouble, but mostly I kept to myself. I slept under bridges, got hot meals at pantry lines, and wallowed in sorrow. That all changed when I returned home to Lyons, and a stranger happened to gift me a ticket to the local opera house for the showing of L'Africaine (The African Woman).

***

The Nouvel Opera House of Lyons was built in 1756, then replaced in 1831, and this would be my first time attending. It would change my life. It would be a cultural experience to which I was unaccustomed. As the evening approached for the performance, I cleaned up the best I could, finding a proper jacket in a charity shop and some dress shoes. The curtain call was 6:45 p.m.

During intermission, I moved about the lobby admiring the paintings and all the decor. The craftsmanship of the opera house was perfection. Hard to believe how the papers labeled it "undistinguished." The builders, Antoine-Marie Chenavard and Jean-Marie Pollet, designed an exquisite theatre with a horseshoe-shaped auditorium and tiers of boxes. It should have been labeled "an architectural tour de force."

Stepping back to take a more generous view of a painting brushed by a local artist is when I bumped into a lady. She was wearing a pearl white gown, with matching arm length gloves, brunette hair tied up in the back and laced with a twig of cream-colored flowers, and she had about her a charm one could easily deduce from any distance. Her parents accompanied her at this performance—I found out later that her father was a well-known merchant in the leather business, and her mother was quite popular in the social circles (although instead of tea, she drank wine).

"Beg my pardon, Madam," I said, turning around and being taken in by this young lady's eyes. They captured me, and I could not look in any other direction. " I'm sorry."

"It's quite all right," she said with a slight smile.

Her voice was hypnotic, soft in tone and I stood there lost in her beauty. "Please forgive me," I said. "I'm Johnathan Laurent, of Lyons. And with whom do I have this delight of being cordial with?"

She blushed ever so slightly. "I'm Catharine."

"Catharine. What a lovely name."

"And this," she said, "is my father and dear mother."

Her father, dressed in a tux, stepped forward and extended his arm. I gripped his hand firmly, "Pierre Fournier," he said in an austere tone.

"Pleasure, sir."

"And this is my wife, Margaret."

"I see now where Catharine gets her beauty from." I took hold of Margaret's hand and placed a soft kiss upon it.

And that is how I met Catharine Fournier. From the moment I turned around, I fell in love with her. In that instant, that moment, that very second our eyes locked onto each other, I knew she was to be mine.

After the performance, I found her again in the crowd of theater-goers. I asked Pierre if I could accompany his lovely daughter to dinner for the upcoming Friday evening. He granted his permission with a slight nod.

That Friday evening came, and I met Catharine at the La Ampere Bistro, one of the finest eateries in all of

France. Luckily, I had been hired as a helper for two days doing general labor and earned eight Francs. Our meal was splendid, and we took to the park adjacent to the levee for a night stroll. Catharine was sophisticated, well-read, elegant, and strikingly beautiful. The moment my hand slipped into hers, I felt I was destined to be with her.

"I must say, amongst all the stars and moon, you are the one illuminating my heart."

She squeezed my hand. "Jonathan, look," she said, pointing toward the vast sky. A single star shot across the liquid black curtain of the world. "Quick, make a wish."

I closed my eyes and wished for a lifetime with her. To call her my wife and be with her until my last breath was to be expelled. After the star blazed into the darkness, I leaned toward her and placed a soft kiss on her cheek.

"You are my only wish," I said as we continued our walk.

I escorted her home, ten minutes before her curfew, and we said our brief farewells. I placed a kiss upon her hand and headed out along the gravel pathway, thinking of her beauty, and when I'd see her again.

A month later, I asked Pierre if I could have Catharine's

hand in marriage. At first, he declined, but later, he relinquished, saying, "I'll let you marry my daughter, only when you provide me with three letters of reference regarding your character. And, of course, how you plan on providing for her."

This I couldn't do. I knew of no one who could bear witness to my nature. When I got to thinking of who I knew, I had no family or colleagues; I felt invisible. There was no circle of friends; it was just me and my prayer book. My employment was as unsteady as walking the bow of a boat.

When I told Pierre I had no references to my character, he said, "For your humbleness, I will be your benefactor. You have good character and employment."

"Employment?" I questioned.

"You will work for me."

✲✲✲

Sir Pierre Fournier was the lead partner with Cuir et Mercantile (Leather & Mercantile). The business was started by his father and his father before him. It was a staple industry in Lyons and sat on the outskirts of the village.

In 1855, the leather business was prosperous. Trade

and export were flourishing, and Pierre put me through a two month business class, then I took charge of investing all the company's returns. In late 1856, the economy crashed. Businesses shut their doors, trading came to a standstill, and the freight industry now required monies before leaving port, which companies could not afford as they received no payment until the delivery of the product.

One month before the crash, I invested heavily in exporting one hundred containers of leather, which never left port. Thus, our customers never received their orders and canceled existing contracts with Cuir dt Mercantile. The company went bankrupt thirty-five days later.

I not only lost my job and reputation, but I cost Pierre his business, his reputation, his friends, and his social standing. He was now shunned in public, and I was the cause. I also lost the dream of having Catharine's hand in marriage.

With the loss of her, my soul broke. I felt it tear and disappear. My life was nothing without her. My mind became fragile. I could no longer contain a thought. I had no future.

I sank back into my wandering vagabond days. Traveling back to the city of Paris, I contemplated jumping into the Seine behind the Louvre Museum. Maybe the river could wash all this pain away, cleanse the hurt and purify my soul once again.

Time vanished. I didn't know the day or hour. My clothes were dirty, the hair on my face was thick and unkempt, and I began to mumble and stammer in my speech. I decided to no longer communicate with the people of Paris or anyone else. Hours under bridges were spent reading my prayer book and babbling about my shattered soul. Tears welled in my eyes at the thought of Catharine and how I longed to hold her hand once more or share a stroll through the park or indulge in one of our conversations at a small bistro in the village. But she was gone. My heart burned, realizing she was probably in the company of another gentleman by now.

When the weather brought about coldness and shorter days, I knew a season of depression was coming. I caught a newspaper headline warning of an unusual wind pattern that would push Paris into the coldest winter. "Arctic Winds Will Blow Into Paris," it read. The paper was dated 24 October 1857.

That night, authorities did a sweep of the city and rounded up all the vagrants. As they questioned me, I could only respond in incoherent mumbles and gestures. Oddly, one monsieur of the police nationale recognized me.

"*Look who we got here,*" *he said to his partner.* "*It's Jonathan Laurent.*"

"*The Cuir et Mercantile who ruined Sir Fournier?*"

"*Oui, oui.*"

"*Sad story. Sir Fournier lost his fortune, then his fille, Catharine.*"

Lost Catharine? My heart plunged deeper into darkness. My body was in knots as if soured with poisonousness food. Catharine, my love, my everything was gone. My heart fractured into pieces. She was lost. Forever.

★★★

The police nationale had me committed to the asile de fous for the mentally unstable. My evenings were spent lashing out, hollering for Catharine. I began to claw my flesh until I drew blood. I needed to feel the pain I had inflicted upon Sir Fournier and Catharine. I was forbidden to have writing utensils, glass, string, a mirror; I had no possessions except my prayer book, furniture, and a naked bed. Everything from me had been stripped away. It did not matter, for my will to live was gone.

I prayed for God to take me during my sleep and bring me to the palace of eternal slumber. Let my spirit dance again with Catharine, even if for just one dance, one step, one twirl. My mind continuously flashed portraits of her and replayed the evening I met her at the Nouvel Opera House of Lyons.

During the day, I walked about the courtyard, clutching my prayer book, mumbling prayers under my breath, and holding conversations with Catharine as if she were beside me. I wandered through the garden in the same pattern for hours. Sometimes I prayed for the sun to scorch my soul for what I've done, and in the coldness of winter, I wished for my heart to freeze. This was to be my routine for the next two years. I never spoke to the staff or other patients committed for an array of reasons.

In late 1858, I decided to escape this madness and impose a penance upon myself. I waited for the winter to pass and continued with my daily routine. In the spring of 1859, I had a strategy for my exit.

There was an extensive blockade near the garden gate that obstructed the view from the facility's front. Roll call was not made until well after dinner, after we had retreated to our quarters. This, I knew, would give me a three-hour head start. When the staff member blew the whistle for us to file back in, I ducked behind the wall. One nurse looked about the courtyard, then closed the door.

I made my way along Blanc Street, where I stole some clothes hanging from a line and threw away the white gown I had been issued. From there, I proceeded down the neighboring village and sat on a bench near the docks. Once nightfall approached, I stowed away on the Castiglione, sharing my cramped space with rats and a foul stench.

I was heading to America.

The Old Leatherman's Diary
Part II

The voyage to America was rough, and I would only move about the vessel during the night, making sure I was undetected and steal small portions of food and drink. I was cold, lonely, and empty inside. I got no sunlight, no warmth, no ocean breeze, just a dark, dingy hole in the ship's hull for the duration.

The two-month voyage took a toll on my stomach; a combination of seasickness and being malnourished caused me to dry heave more than once. My soul rejoiced for a moment when I heard the first mate, holler, "Land ho!" The words brought me joy and greater sorrow. I could hear the shouts of happiness and the roar of excitement as we finally arrived in America, but my Catherine would never greet me there.

Three days later, we docked in what I later learned was Philadelphia, a prominent city in the state of

Pennsylvania. I stayed hunkered down and remained hidden in the hull until nightfall. When all was quiet, I then disembarked from the Castiglione—wandering along the main thoroughfare of the village, where I rummaged for bits of food.

Hearing of stories about New York, I eventually wanted to make my trek northeastward. The streets of Philadelphia were nothing like Lyons or Paris. The cobblestone lanes made walking a challenge, and the buildings failed compared to my home country's elegance.

During my first night in America, I walked through Fairmount Park. By daybreak, I was tired but no longer hungry. Not far from the park was the Hopewell & Burns Leather Company. I scrounged through the scrap containers out back and began to sew a large leather suit. This would not only provide me with protection from the elements of Mother Nature, it would also give me my name along my journey—The Leatherman. I also sewed together some smaller scraps and made a pouch attached to the end of a stick.

I didn't mind the name of Leatherman, but one village referred to me as the man "dressed in a cowhide suit," which was less to my liking.

By high noon, the city was bustling. People flooded the market with their meats and fish, and children skipped rope and shot marbles. I knew a quieter place to serve my penance was upstate New York and was anxious to arrive there.

It took me a month to make my trek to New York. East of what they call the Hudson River, I found a shallow cave, where I could rest and build a small fire. In my new destination, my first night was a restful evening, but still, no matter how much time lapses, I missed Catharine. The softness of her voice and the passion of her kiss. It would be the first of many nights I'd cry myself to sleep.

When the sun woke me in the early morning hours, I felt rested. After a few days hibernating in a cave east of the Hudson, I began my trek in April 1859. Ten days later, I was in New Haven, Connecticut.

This town would become a regular stop for me. The townsfolk were friendly and offered me food and drink. I quickly learned my way through the small towns and villages along the Hudson, and eventually, I made a loop, which took me thirty-four days to complete.

After a few more times of wandering through the villages, the press began to report of my so-called visits. The more often I'd pass through a village, the more press I tended to receive. One paper described me as: "A Frenchman, aged about 35 years, dressed entirely in leather, stripped from old bootlegs, etc., and who carries a leather pack on his back and a tin pail in his hand, continually travels about the country, coming from the same direction and passing through the fields at a certain point."

Another publication wrote, "It is not known where he came from, but it is generally supposed that he escaped from some Dime Novel." And yet another described me as "very greasy and ill adored." Lastly, another stated I was an "uncouth, repulsive, and wholly inexplicable person who has loomed up in certain localities to puzzle the good people of these sections."

The local rag Connecticut Valley Advertiser reported: "Once more struck queerly upon our vision as with unwashed aspect and serious mien he passed silently by on Main Street, headed South, as he invariably heads in all his journeys through Deep River."

I was surprised by all the attention I gathered simply wandering through a town. Over the years, nicknames for me have been recorded as Old Leatherman, O'Leathery, Odd-Looking Mortal, Queer Old Chap, Tramp, and I've been compared to the Wandering Jew and Bret Hart's famous "Heathen Chinee."

None of these reporters ever questioned me. They made up fanciful stories to please their editors and readers.

Children loved to hand me pennies, which I placed

on the fence posts as I left their family farms. I found this county's women gracious and seemed somewhat humbled and proud when they fed me. Some would offer me a piece of apple pie or fruit, while others served up an entire meal fit for a king. Most men tried to converse with me when I came through their towns, but I was one of few words, plus there was a language barrier. I know they just wanted to know who I was and what my story was, but I could never figure out why. What's so important they had to know about me? After all, I was just a harmless wanderer passing through one footstep at a time.

Three years into my penance, America broke out into a war against itself. North vs. South, the War Between States it was called.

In 1861, I noticed a bunch of young men gathering on the green in New Haven, Connecticut. One man stood on a platform hollering through a megaphone to the assembled group. "Boys, the time has come to unite all states under one government. Our president, Abraham Lincoln, is asking each and every one of you to put aside your business, say goodbye for a time to your family, and forge ahead with what will be a new nation and stronger country!" The crowd of boys gave a heartfelt cheer, then fell into line and began to march along the main street toward the train depot. They seemed eager enough, as they had no idea what they were in for. No one noticed me as I trudged on by with my leather sack *slung over my shoulder.*

I've known from my father's experience that war is hell. The blood, the mayhem, the atrocities of macabre, and the sight of a fellow soldier dying in excruciating pain is much to bear.

The papers were full of horror stories of this war between the states. It appears Lincoln and the Union want the Confederate States to join their cause that all states should be united. My gut told me it was going to be a long war.

As I continued my trek south toward New York, one boy, in full uniform, asked me for a match. I pulled out a box of wooden matchsticks from my pouch and lit his smoke for him. "Thanks," he said, blowing out a cloud of gray smoke. "Where ya headed?"

I made a gesture I was going to continue south.

"Cat got your tongue?" he asked, inhaling another puff.

I began to walk away from him when he grabbed me by the arm and turned me around. "You're not a polite fella, are ya?" I again gestured that I needed to head south. "Why are you in such a hurry? Can you talk?"

I grunted a few times while pointing at my mouth.

"Oh, I see," the soldier said. "You're a mute of some kind, aren't ya?"

I agreed with him by nodding.

"I see. Well, as you can tell, I'm heading off to the war, and I'll tell ya; frankly, I'm scared. I mean, I don't want people shooting at me, and I even got some cousins down south. How can I ever take potshots at them? My momma cried up a storm as I left, ya know. Can't blame her. I'm the only son left. My two brothers died in a farming accident."

I could tell the kid was nervous, talking a mile a minute. I could see and hear the fear rise in him. Silently I said a prayer that God may watch over him and bring him back to his mother.

"Hey, look, I need to get going, ya know. My country needs me right now. Maybe I'll run into you again some time."

I nodded, then restarted my trek southward. I glanced back and saw the young soldier walking toward the depot.

***

Later that night, I made it to the Connecticut/New

York state line. Not far from the main route, there was a small cave where I spent time. That night, I recalled my mother telling me of my father's time in the war. She didn't say a great deal; I guess the burden of memories were too much to bear.

I wondered if the burden is equal to what I now carry? Every night I prayed for Catharine's voice to speak to me. To whisper that it's all a bad dream. Instead, I would be woken up by the sunlight, a hungry stomach, or sometimes by a squirrel or another rodent sniffing me.

I chose to stay along the Hudson River and small towns throughout Connecticut as they saw none of the war. Most of the battles were fought in the southern territory. Unlike the soldiers fighting in the campaign, I had my own action to worry about.

One afternoon, a few gentlemen thought it best if they loosened my tongue with some whiskey. As two men held me down, a third poured a quarter of a bottle of non-top shelf poison down my gullet. I spit out as much of it as I could. They gave up and let me go without me speaking a word. I discovered later they denied the whole ordeal when questioned by authorities. I resumed my travels, altered my trek to never walk down that path again.

The winter seasons were brutal with the sub-zero

temps, snow, icy rain, and blustery winds. Then the summers were filled with hazy, hot, humid days, yet I never took off my suit of leather. Spring and fall were usually mild, comfortable, and good hiking weather. I began to leave some kindling wood at each cave, and in a few places, I was able to grow a small garden and harvested tomatoes, lettuce, and carrots.

In 1877, the Woodbury Reporter ran an op-ed piece by Alexander Gordon, Jr., part-owner of the Gordon Tannery. We've never spoken, but he was kind enough to oil my leather to the amount of two quarts for which he never asked for a penny. Somehow, he thought he had me figured out. It was an amusing read.

"I will give you a short sketch of his birth. Twenty-five years ago, the person known as the 'Leatherman' lived in a thriving village in western New York. He carried on a large and profitable business as a tanner and currier, and was considered a prosperous and wealthy man. He owned a splendid mansion, beautiful grounds, horses, carriages, and servants at [his] command, and all of this world's goods the heart could desire. Then a sudden change came over him. An incendiary fire destroyed his manufacturing establishment, together with his dwelling; the lady to whom he was engaged died about the same time. These combined losses unseated his reason, and he became a wanderer over earth, seeking for his lost love and loss of his youth. Twice a year he visits her grave, covers it with flowers, then on his *weary round he goes."*

What rubbish. And they wonder why I choose a vow of silence.

On one occasion, in 1885, I crossed the threshold of a door and entered an establishment. Mr. Sarrow, who owned the local general store, beckoned for me to come in. I took a seat beside the stove to warm up, and he was gentleman enough to supply me with crackers and cheese. He asked for my age, of which I did not answer. Finally, he said, "I am old," and scribbled a number on a sheet of paper. "How old are you?"

He handed me the paper. I slowly wrote 15342 and handed it back to him. Little did I realize this would cause a great conundrum amongst the inhabitants of the village. Some figured I was born on the 15th day, of the third month, in 1842. Others twisted it to be I'd be turning 42 on March 15, and perhaps the most insane thought is that I am a man of 15,342 years of age.

The Old Leatherman's Diary
Part III

I was pleased to read the war between the states had finally ended. A nerve in me twitched when I thought of the war as it reminded me of my father.

By late April, I was again crossing the Scranton

Farm. I've grown accustomed to Marion's fine cooking, which usually came with a half-bottle of wine. As has been par since the start of the war, she was alone. I came up to the front porch where she was seated. She excused herself and came back out with a hot meal.

"Here you go," she said, placing the dish in front of me on top of an old wooden barrel. "Hope it's to your liken. It's potatoes, bread, some meat, and fresh lettuce from the garden."

I nodded as I cut into the meat, putting a relatively large bite into my mouth. Right then, a breeze kicked up, and music could be heard from the few wind chimes hanging in the far corner of the porch.

"You know, you're a legend in these parts. You're always getting written up in the press."

I continued with my meal, only grunting a couple of times to convey I enjoyed the food.

"What's it like?" she asked me.

I looked at her.

"What's it like to wander all day? To trudge through town after town, never knowing where your next meal is coming from? Don't you get cold during the winter months?"

Placing my fork down, I pointed to my leather.

"Well, that's good for wind and rain, but what about the cold? Sometimes Mother Nature likes to lower the temp down to what I consider unnatural." She stared at me as I finished my potatoes. "You certainly don't talk much. All the papers say you're a French man. Is that true?"

I nodded.

"Well, now I'm getting somewhere. Why did you come here? To America?"

Using my index finger, I drew a circle around my chest then made the gesture of something being broke.

"You have a broken heart? So, you came here to escape the sorrow?"

I nodded again.

"Were you married?"

I pointed to my ring finger and shook my head.

"You seem to understand English. Do you understand what I'm saying?"

I nodded.

"So, you understand the language, just refuse to speak it?"

This time, I bowed my head, made a few gestures to thank her for the meal, and began to leave her porch. As I tossed my hobo stick and sack over my shoulder, she stood in front of me.

"Stay a while longer. Won't you?"

I indicated that I needed to continue on my route.

"My husband's been gone since the war started. This is my parents' land and farm, and they aren't around anymore. I have no neighbors and could use some company. It's all right if you don't talk. Just listen."

Tears welled up in her eyes. I knew better than anyone what loneliness was. I looked down the path that leads back to the dirt road, then turned and looked back at her porch.

"Please."

Putting my leather sack on the porch beside a stool, she opened the front door and invited me in. I pointed to the chair instead and sat down.

"Or, I guess, we can chat out here." She pulled her chair up next to mine. "I haven't heard from my husband in over five months. I'm beginning to believe the war swallowed him. No letter or visit from the government, none of his comrades have come around, and I check the church bulletin every Sunday for an update, but there's been nothing."

It appears what she needed was a listener; I could provide. She spoke with such compassion, her voice radiant and soothing, like that of a mother wooing her child in a time of need. She began to remind me of Catharine. Although, Catharine wouldn't have run a farm on her own.

From what I figured, Marion had a deep desire to be comforted. I slowly reached my hand out and placed it on top of hers, which was resting on her thigh. I nodded a few times, letting her know I understood. At least she had the chance of her love returning. He might one day, hopefully soon, walk out from the woods returning from the South and be back in her arms.

She took my hand and examined it. "You know what, you could use a good cleaning. When was the last time you had a bath?"

With my other hand, I held up four fingers.

"Four days?"

I shook my head.

"Four weeks?"

I shook my head again.

"Four months? Four months since you've bathed. I think we need to get you to the barn. Why don't you head over there while I warm up some water?"

I made my way over to the barn and past three horse stalls where a large metal tub sat. I undressed, hanging my leather suit on the beam, and sat in the tub. I guess this would count as one of the rare occasions I was inside. Resting my head back and closing my eyes, I could hear Catharine's voice. She was singing. In my mind, I could see her, running through an open prairie, with me chasing her. Her smile was as wide as a river.

"Are ya ready?" a voice asked, startling me from my thoughts.

Marion stood over me with two buckets. Slowly she poured each one in. The water was perfect, warm, refreshing. She also had a cloth and a bar of soap. Wrapping the soap bar into the washcloth, she began to wash my back, neck and worked her way around my front.

"*Well, look at all this dirt comin' off ya,*" *she said.* "*I'm surprised people haven't mistaken ya for a man of color.*" *She went to the corner of the barn and refilled one of the buckets. Coming back to the tub, she poured it over me, washing away all the grime, dirt, and soap.* "*Stand up, old Leatherman,*" *she ordered me.*

I stood up, cold, wet, and stark naked. I had only ever been naked in front of my mother as a child. I moved my hands to cover what I had from her view.

"*You ain't think I ain't seen some manhood before? Please,*" *she said, wrapping a white towel around me.* "*Why don't ya step out, dry off.*"

She watched me as I finished drying off.

"*Can I tell ya sometin'?*"

I nodded.

"*I don't think Jake, that'd be my husband, is coming back. I figure if he were, he'd be home by now. The war ended a month ago.*"

I glanced over at my leather.

"*Ya know, I thought before ya put on that suit of yours, why don't we get to know each other better.*

I bet it's been a long time since you got to know a woman."

All of a sudden, she began to sing in a soft voice. She took a step toward me, grabbed my hand, and placed my other hand on her waist. We started to sway, and she pulled me closer, still singing.

"The heart grows fond,
My mind remembers a lot
When you were gone,
I had you, and it was for not."

I couldn't place the lyrics or the melody.

"When was the last time you kissed a woman, Leatherman?"

I put my head down and took a step back. She reached into her apron pocket and pulled out a leaf.

"Here. Chew on this, it will fresh'n that breath of yours."

I took the mint leaf and gave it a sniff before putting it in my mouth. The mint flavor raced around my mouth and smelled good. She then took a step toward me.

"Don't be shy. It's only you and me. As I said, it's been a while for you, and my husband has yet to return or write. I feel maybe the worst has happened."

She pulled me back into her, and we continued to sway about the barn floor while she kept singing this unfamiliar tune:

"When two hearts meet
They become one.
When two hearts beat,
They stay as one."

Then it happened. She locked her lips with mine. It was not the same as kissing Catharine. My heart didn't skip a beat; I didn't want more. Marion's kiss was commanding. She waltzed me over to a stall full of loose hay and pushed me down. Standing over me, she removed her shirt, then her hoop skirt, followed by her chemise and drawers. I hadn't seen a naked woman before.

Marion laid on top of me, pressing her body against mine. I immediately became aroused when her hand found its way between my legs. We kissed passionately, but not like lovers. My hands explored her body, as did my lips and tongue. I suckled on her breasts and pressed my fingers between her thighs. Our conversation was now moaning and groaning. She positioned herself on top of me, taking all that I had for manhood inside her, letting out a gasp of excitement. She kept me pinned down until we hit our climax together. After absorbing the feeling of satisfaction, she rolled off of me and laid beside me in the hay.

"I hope ya come by more often," she said in between a few pants.

I laid still, breathing heavily. As soon as we were finished, my thoughts went to Catharine. Even though she's gone, I felt a wave of guilt rush through me.

Marion ran her fingers through my chest hair and nuzzled up beside me. I made a few grunts and stood up. "After all that, ya leavin'? Thought ya'd be more of a man than that."

I began to put my leather back on, ready to return to my trek.

"Hold on a sec. Don't go just yet," she said, getting dressed and then heading back into her house. She returned a couple of minutes later. "Here. He won't be needing these." She threw a pair of long underwear and an undershirt at me. "Try and stay warm at night." She then turned and walked back into her house.

I stuffed the extra clothing into my sack and walked out of the barn. On the front porch, she left me some food as well. I waited another minute, but Marion never came back out.

***

Thirty-four days later, I returned to the Scranton farm, but no one was there. It looked like the fields hadn't been plowed, and the wind chimes were gone. The place was eerily quiet. I wandered up to the front porch and noticed the barrel and stools were gone. Making my way to the barn, the horse stalls were empty, including the one where Marion and I had embraced a month ago.

Gone, I said to myself. I sat on the stoop for a few minutes eating some bread found in my hobo pack, then continued on my path to the next town and then the next farm.

I never returned to the Scranton farm.

The Old Leatherman's Diary
Part IV

In the fall of 1887, authorities from the city of Hartford took me in and placed me in a hospital. The doctors immediately confirmed I had throat cancer, and it had spread to my lower lip, causing an abnormality to grow. They bombarded me with questions, all of which I had heard over the years. What's your name? Do you speak English? Where are you from? Do you have any family we can contact?

My answer to all of these questions was the same: silence.

This would be the only time I stayed indoors since that day in the barn. I needed to get out. Although the cancer on my lower lip was painful, I needed to get back to my solitary wandering. On my second day there, after the evening nurse made her rounds, I snuck out of the room, found my worldly possessions, and continued serving my penance. They never bothered me again.

People were becoming more accustomed to me passing through. Many would wave and shout a friendly "hello." Lately, there has been a lot of hype about a contraption called a camera, and some had taken it upon themselves to snap this at me. Not sure what the purpose of that was, but it is nothing I could control.

The winter of 1887 into early 1888 was bitter cold. My leather suit, stuffed with newspapers and an old coat, hardly kept the bite of arctic weather at bay. Small fires in the caves provided little heat but were essential for my cooking when I was far from a farm or town to beg for a meal. The cave shelters kept the wind to a minimum but did nothing for the cold.

The winter of 1888 just about did me in. It was bitter cold, complete with frostbite. The growth on my lip was becoming larger with every passing day, and my body ached. My pace slowed considerably. I needed more rest, but I also knew my penance was coming to an end, so I trudged along.

Soon I'd rest peacefully. I would pray that my eternal sleep would bring me back to Catharine. That our spirits could dance, and our souls connect as they did when we were mortals here on earth. She was all I wanted. To have her heartbeat beside mine would have made me a whole man. I've often heard that God has a plan, but sometimes you never learn what His plan is.

While I don't fear death, I do question when. When will my heart stop? When will God decided my penance has been paid?

I thought that time had arrived when I awoke on March 11, 1888, and found that I was buried in snow in my cave. Winds were howling, and I could hear branches snapping in half. I had no choice but to hunker down and wait out the storm.

Luckily, I had some bread, a quart of beer, and some dried fruit as it would be three days before I could tunnel out.

***

It was a challenging walk into town, which looked like it had been painted white. Only a handful of people were out and about. The rails had stopped, and not a single horse and carriage was seen.

Mr. Leffler's Coffee House, however, was open.

"You look like you could use a cup of hot coffee," a stranger said to me.

I showed him my pocket was empty.

"That's all good and well," he said. "On a cold day like this, it will be my treat. Nothing in return."

I nodded in thanks and remained outside while he went in. A minute later, he returned with a cup with some steaming coffee in it, and a saucer. The heat of the cup against my lower lip felt comforting, for I believe it was now completely frozen. I took a few small sips, then nodded once again to the gentleman.

"Good day to you, sir. Keep warm," he said, heading off in the opposite direction.

Looking ahead, I knew the snowfall would severely hamper the next few days of walking. Roads had not been cleared and indeed not the paths I'd been accustomed to following.

The cold weather played tricks on my mind, and I began to hallucinate. As I reached the outskirts of town, I thought I saw Catharine. She looked as charming as she did the day I met her. I made a loud gurgle sound as I tried to holler her name. She turned around and stared at me, almost like she recognized me.

It's me, Catharine, I said. However, I didn't say it out loud. I tried to holler once again for her, but my mouth did not cooperate. It's me! I'm here, Catharine. I'm right here.

I fell to the ground with my arm and hand reaching out to her. When I looked up, she was gone. I got up and looked in every direction, but she was nowhere. I got to where she was standing and realized there was only snow. No footprints. She was never here. Yet, she looked so alive. I only wanted to hold her hand, to tell her how much I loved her still.

I gathered myself together and continued. My secret hope is she would come back, that she would come back and tell me how her heart is all mine, how she has been missing me as I've been missing her.

As the sun began to break through the overcast sky, I felt that perhaps the snow would start to melt.

***

I was only able to trudge six miles today, versus my usual ten. This meant I needed to find a new shelter for the night. With the impossibility of finding any caves,

I rested by nestling myself between some boulders. The ground was cold, but the wind was gone. By morning, my body ached, but I slowly continued on my trek, keeping an eye out for Catharine.

I would be glad when this winter was over.

***

Going into 1889 was cold, but eventually, I got back to my regular 34-day route. By mid-March, I could feel a change in my body. It was tiring, sore, and my lower lip felt as if it were going to fall off; part of me hoped it would.

When I arrived at the farm of George Dell, he gave me a hot meal and a bottle of beer, which I took to the cave that sat on his property.

Was my penance worth it? Have I done the right thing? I've given my life to suffer for the wrong I did, and now I wonder if I've suffered enough.

As I laid down, my only thought was of Catharine. I choose this penance, for I have wronged Catharine, her father, and family. This leather suit reminds me of the burden I caused their family. Just a few days ago, my father came to me.

"Son," he said, standing at the entrance of the cave.

"Let go. We are all here."

He looked like how I remembered him in his uniform before going off to war. Seeing him made me feel like a nine-year-old lad once again. I wanted to play ball with him and tell him stories.

"Where's mother?"

"She's here, son. We are all here, waiting for you."

He began to look blurry and faded away.

"Father," I managed to yell, which placed incredible pain on my lip, causing me to cough.

The cough never ceased from that day on and wreaked havoc on my throat. Drinking and eating became intolerable, and my sleep was interrupted by coughing fits. As the weather finally began to warm up, my body went from shivering to sweating.

Is this how death arrives? Is this how my soul travels to the next dimension? Will I be doomed to repeat a penance once again? Am I going to be damned to hell, or will I sit next to Our Father? Is it true that there is a warm reception of all the souls I knew before waiting to greet me and bring me into their cluster?

I could hear farmer Dell and his horses plowing the

field in the distance, readying it for planting season.

Rummaging through my sack, I pulled out my prayer book. I turned to Isaiah 25:8. "He will swallow up death forever. The Sovereign LORD will wipe away the tears from all faces; he will remove his people's disgrace from all the earth."

Does this mean I will be changing in my leather for wings? Can He genuinely wipe away my disgrace, all my silent tears from the years of a burden I've chosen to carry?

"You in here?" spoke a voice.

Is that God, I wondered. Is he here? Am I going?

"Brought ya a hot meal."

It was farmer Dell. With all the energy I could muster, I leaned forward, nodded my head, and took the plate. He quickly returned to his horses and plow. Farmer Dell was always kind to me.

On the plate was an ear of corn cob, a potato, an apple, and a few nuts and berries. My last meal, I thought. Through the discomfort of swallowing, I managed to eat most of the food and regained a bit of strength, but not nearly enough to walk.

I laid back down thinking of Catharine, as I had often done throughout my life, throughout my penance. Holding my good book up, I flipped the pages to 1 Corinthians 15:42-44. "So will it be with the resurrection of the dead. The body that is sown is perishable, it is raised imperishable; it is sown in dishonor, it is raised in glory; it is sown in weakness, it is raised in power; it is sown a natural body, it is raised a spiritual body. If there is a natural body, there is also a spiritual body."

My spiritual body, I thought. What became of my spirit? I feel that I broke it a long time ago. I felt the connection of my spiritual body with Catharine's the day we met. It was as if they collided. Our spirits began to dance that evening at the opera house. They created their own music and passion. There was nothing, I felt, Catharine or I could not have done together. We were pulled as one by our spirits, for they knew they could no longer be separated.

But it was a brief dance. Our spirits were ripped apart by my actions. Then her spirit was taken home while mine was left to the elements of which I loaded on it, putting on such a strain from which it could never recover.

Does it return when it's time to travel? When it's time to make the transition, will it be here? I can't rightfully blame my spirit if it never comes back. But

God, my God, the God I believe in, is all-forgiving and will accept me.

I closed my eyes, clutched my prayer book to my chest, and laid down on the cold ground. Sleep was elusive these past few days. How strange that a tired human cannot fall asleep. All for the better; perhaps being awake will keep the dreams away. Yet, being awake for days on end plays tricks with the mind. I've already seen my father, and before that, my dear Catharine. I swear by my flesh and blood I saw her. She looked right at me, the same way she did that night at the opera house.

I'm not sure if this journal will ever be found, but please note this was just the life of a lonely, heartbroken, French man, serving a self-imposed penance.

Suivre mes pas, c'est connaitre mon ame (To follow in my footsteps is to know my soul.)

The Legend

"The Leatherman is dead! The Leatherman is dead!" shouted two kids running down the street toward pedestrians and store owners. The newspaper boy on the corner was hollering, *"Extra! Extra! Read all about it! Leatherman found dead in a cave!"*

As strangely as he appeared from nowhere, he was gone. Gone for good and leaving no clue as to who he was and what his story was about.

Reports stated the Leatherman was a wanted criminal who had escaped from the authorities in Hartford, Connecticut and disguised himself in a suit of leather to avoid being recognized. Although it was never mentioned what crime he committed. Rumors spread like wildfire. Another report stated he was hiding from debt collectors, faked his death, and his wife collected on the insurance, but their scheme was uncovered. One paper even wrote the Leatherman was a spy sent from the southern states before the war. According to the article, his objective was to collect gossip among small towns and learn how they felt about their government, their viewpoints on slavery, and who was involved in the underground railroad.

Only Albert Dowd would learn the truth of the Leatherman after his mother sat down her twenty-one-year-old son. She poured him a tall glass of lemonade and sat across from him at the small round table on their front porch. "Albert," she said, drawing in a deep breath, "your Pa has been gone now for three years. He loved you very much."

"I know, Ma."

"Well," she stared off into the field that laid up to the thickly wooded area. "I need to share something with you ... Pa... well... he wasn't your Pa."

Albert almost choked on his lemonade. "What do you mean? Sure he is. He raised me and taught everything 'bout farming and hunt'n."

"I know he did, son. But there is something neither

you nor your Pa ever knew."

They both sat in a moment of silence, each wondering what the other was thinking.

"Well, what it be?"

She blew out a deep breath. "When your Pa went off to war, I was left here all alone. Not a neighbor or family member to speak of. Then one day, a gentleman happened to be strolling through our farm. He was hungry, so I fed him some of my good home cook'n. Then, he went on his way only to return the follow'n month, the month after that, and so on. I would feed him a nice home-cooked meal each time. Finally, one day I learned he had a broken heart. I could see the misery that swallowed him from losing her.

"He was lonely; I could see it in his eyes. He missed her as much as I was missing your Pa. Upon each of his visits, I cooked a much larger meal so that he'd stay for a spell longer. There was never much conversation between us. It was like we spoke with our eyes, and it felt as if our hearts, maybe our souls, were engaging with one another.

"After dinner one evening, he stayed well beyond his usual time. I sang some songs, and he teared up. As I leaned toward him to wipe away these tears, which I'm sure were memories for him, I felt this pull. As if my soul needed to be touched by him. He removed his leather garb and embraced me.

"It had been so long since I'd been held, and I haven't heard from your Pa in months. I started to believe the war took him."

"Why are you telling me this, Ma?"

"Because the Leatherman who was discovered dead this morning was your father," Marion said. "Your Pa, well, he finally did come home from the war after the Union declared victory. Before that, I thought he had given his life for our great country. I could feel that I was with child, and I never told him. That is, I never told the Leatherman about you because I never did see him again and never told your Pa about him either. He spent his last eighteen years raising you as his own because he never knew."

Albert sat motionless. "The old Leatherman is my real Pa?"

"It's true," Marion said.

Albert took a sip of his now warm lemonade. "How come I've never seen him come around? According to the tales, he always walked the same circuit."

"I insisted to your Pa that we move immediately upon his return. The war was over, and we should find another farm to call our own and raise our son. Of course, my main reason was I didn't want the Leatherman coming by and seeing your Pa or you.

"If the Leatherman was to look into your eyes, why he'd see himself and know for sure who you were. I just couldn't chance that. I couldn't let your Pa know, and I couldn't let you know until now. You're old enough to know the truth."

Albert looked out into the field then up toward the sky. "I want to know about my Pa, my real Pa," he said, turning to face his mother.

"I'm afraid there's not much to tell, son. I only know that he was in love and then had his heartbroken. It tore him to pieces, so he left France, according to most accounts, and came to America where he spent the last forty years or so just wandering and keeping his thoughts to himself. A few reports mentioned that he worked for a brief time in a leather company, but other than that, I know nothing of him."

"There has to be someone who knows more. Maybe there was a French-speaking person along his route, and they shared a conversation."

"I'm sure if there was, the paper would have written about it. After all, he was somewhat of a legend."

"I still want to know," Albert said, standing up and once again looking out to the farmland, which stretched for a half-mile until it intersected with a dirt road.

"Oh, Albert, I can tell what you're thinking, and I don't like it one bit. I need you here."

"I need to know my Pa, my real Pa."

"Albert Dowd, if you leave here, who will do the harvest?"

"I'll go after the harvest. I'll go to the Dell Farm and then follow in his footsteps. I'll retrace his route and meet the people he met. Someone must know somethin'. They just have too."

"Albert, son, you're only setting yourself up for disappointment. No one knew him. I'm probably the only one who got some information out of him, and I surely couldn't go to the paper and share it." She stood up and cleared the empty glasses, and headed back inside.

***

In late October, with the harvest over, Albert stood at the front stoop and bid his mother goodbye. "I'll be back in thirty-four days, mother. I promise."

"You be careful out there, son."

Albert squinted, looking into the sun that rose above their house. "If my Pa can wander this route for forty years, I'm sure I can do it once." With that, he turned and took the first step of his journey to discover his father—The Old Leatherman.

Ghost Music

Introduction: This short story was first published in Katatim Short Horror Stories Vol. 1 (2017). *I had submitted this piece to a few horror publications in which I received encouragement to rework the beginning but decided to leave it as is (for now). The idea for this story came about after my wife and I had watched a few horror movies.*

The trail began at the edge of the forest, where all the hideous, terrifying scars were left on the town. This is where he came from and often took the lives of those who dared to enter. It was the music, the elders said. He came to town; a dark, broad, heathen is how they referred to him. Like the Pied Piper of Hamelin, he played his eerie music and set the townspeople into a trance. Men left, women cried, and the children followed him right into the forest.

"Cover your ears when you go by the forest," the elders chanted. "You don't want to be one of them."

The forest was lavish, and the music drifted through the trees' thickness as if it knew the way. As I stood still, I could hear the faint melody I've heard previously during a dark time in my life. As it had before, it lured me into the forest. The birds were quiet, and the crickets silent. The air stagnant, humid, and had a scent of staleness to it. The only sound was my bare feet breaking twigs and my heart pounding through my ribcage. In my mind, I could hear all the children who followed him— singing, laughing, and dancing.

The moon gave off only a hint of light, which hindered my navigation through the wild overgrown path, which led to the abandoned, rotting cabin smothered in shiny green moss. The music intensified note by note. As I got closer, the rhythm sounded like a choir of monks, and all of my senses heightened. It was as if the music was going through me, enticing my soul to sing and my spirit to dance. My breathing became faint, short, and dry.

I firmly grasped the cold iron door handle, and then, just like before and as quick as lightning, my mind raced back to a time when I was a child. To a scary place where I tasted fear for the first time. A place I had hoped to forget, but which now came back to me in clear, crisp images. I tried to scream, but nothing vibrated from my hoarse vocal cords. Unable to erase or block this remnant of my past from my mind, I turned the handle and pushed the door inward.

And there he was.

Sitting at his baby grand, producing a sonnet, or a funeral march. His frail, bony fingers barely touched the black and white ivory. He focused on me with his piercing glance. "I've been expecting you," he said in a raspy whisper. "It is time for you to dance." He swiveled in his chair to face the piano. The melody was now hypnotic, and his lyrics were lucent and stirred my soul. "It's time for you to dance," he said again.

I stood frozen with my eyes closed, my knees locked, my fists clenched, and my throat was tasting dry and sore. I couldn't speak, I couldn't move, I couldn't even pray. I didn't want to dance, not with him, not for him, not ever.

Then, the music stopped. An eerie silence fell about the cabin. I could hear him as he stood up from his stool. His breath stunk like stale gin and tobacco, and we were now nose to nose.

"It's time for you to dance," he whispered in my ear, almost touching his lips to my lobe. "It won't hurt, my friend. Well, at least it won't hurt me." With that, he let out a hardy, sinister laugh. He grabbed my left eye lid and pulled it back. "Nurse," he said.

"Wait," I finally managed to say. "I-I-I can dance. A-a-any dance ya want. I'm feel'n much b-b-better."

"Well now," the doctor said, looking down at me. "How remarkable." He let go of my eye lid and gave me a slight laugh with his crooked smile.

With a mighty heave and all my strength, I began to run. But I felt restrained, not putting any distance between us. And like the previous time, and the time before, and the time before that, I woke up tied to a sterile white bed with a monitor blinking and a nurse standing over me handing the doctor an orbitoclast as he once again pulled my eye lid back.

The Devil's Whisper: A Tale of Fate

Introduction: The inspiration for this story came from a quote by Jim Morrison (The Doors). "The Crossroads: A place where ghosts reside to whisper into the ears of travelers & interest them in their fate." It's a stand-alone piece on Amazon.

The Proposal

Although I had rehearsed, my nerves were twisting inside my gut, working overtime. Sweat began to bead across my forehead and ran down along the contours of my face. My heart continued to pound through my chest; even my breathing grew heavy. I never thought I'd see the day I'd be doing this. I glanced at my watch and realized in about ten minutes I would be proposing to Rachael Mathews.

I chose to do this at the Blake Street restaurant, where we had our first date.

I first saw her three years ago at the county carnival. She had gone with two friends. I can't explain what drew me to her, but it felt as if our lives were meant not only to meet but more like collide. It had been a hot—but not humid—July 1st, the carnival's opening day, and I decided to take my eight-year-old nephew to give my sister a much-needed break. He loved the fast rides, funnel cake, and of course, cotton candy.

We were in line for the bumper cars when I saw her exit the ride. I watched her as she walked across the field, heading toward the funhouse. "Wanna make a deal?" I asked my nephew.

"I guess so," he replied.

"How about we skip the bumper cars for now and go to the funhouse?"

"I don't know. I like the bumper cars, and you promised we would go on them."

"I know, but how about we go to the funhouse first, then I buy you another cotton candy. And we can come back to the bumper cars later?"

He turned and twisted his foot in the ground, mulling over my offer. "And popcorn?" he countered.

I couldn't help but laugh. "Yes, we can do popcorn, too."

"Okay." He smiled.

We made our way quickly over to the funhouse just as she got to the entrance. "Excuse me," I said, getting her attention.

"Yes," she said, turning around to face me. For a

second, I froze. Completely out of my comfort zone, I couldn't think of what to say. "Something on your mind?" she asked, as her friends entered the house.

"We're supposed to meet," I said, with a slight crackling in my voice.

"We are, are we? And why is that?"

A long-haired guy with a few tattoos stepped up. "This ain't the place for conversation. Either step aside or go inside."

"May we?" I gestured to her that we would follow her in.

"Be my guest," she said.

We made our way into the hall of mirrors. I felt as if I should check my pulse, as her striking beauty indeed had my heart racing. I was in awe. The mirrors gave view to every angle of her at once. She had shoulder-length, ash blonde hair, an incredible smile, and a body that probably couldn't be in better shape. We made our way through the mirrors onto the uneven floors.

"So, what exactly did you mean, 'We were supposed to meet?'" she asked, trying to keep her balance.

"I'm not sure I can fully explain it."

"Try me. You got this far."

"Well, as soon as you walked in front of me, I felt

like a magnet began pulling me toward you. Like a force, stronger than me, guiding me to follow you. I don't want to freak you out, but a voice whispered to me, 'Go meet her. She's the one.'"

We made our way across the uneven floors to a maze of jail-like bars, weaving in and out.

"Whose voice?"

I stood still for a moment. My nephew entertained himself twirling around the bars and squeezing in between the gaps. "Your mother's," I whispered.

Rachael walked through the spinning tube, not even taking the time to brace her feet, stretch her arms to do a few spins, and exited the funhouse.

"Look, I know that sounds weird, creepy even, but it's true," I said, following her out like a puppy dog. I had no clue where that came from, but I did hear a voice, and, in my gut, I knew it had to be her mother.

"Are we getting cotton candy now?" my nephew asked.

"In a little bit, Buddy."

"How do you know it was my mother? And why would she tell you to follow me?"

"I can't explain how it happened."

Her two friends came out and asked about me.

Rachael said—lied—that I was an old friend and she'd catch up with them in a bit. As they headed toward the Scrambler, she turned back to me and crossed her arms. "I'll give you one more minute of my time to tell me what's going on?"

I looked about the fair, and for a brief second, took in all the attractions, couples walking hand-in-hand, kids running about, and carnival hawkers shouting, "Step right up, you could be a winner!" Then the entire fair suddenly grew quiet, the grounds started to roll like an earthquake, rumbling underneath, and I felt like I drifted into a hypnotic trance. A voice, that same voice, told me to tell her, "She's Rachael Mathews, and she's all that matters."

As I said this out loud, her demeanor changed. She became relaxed. "My mother told me that all the time growing up. How did you know that?"

"She just told me, just as she told me we need to meet."

"I think we should get cotton candy before they close," my nephew said.

I looked at my nephew, then back to her. "Would you like to join us?" I asked, offering her my hand.

She accepted.

***

She turned me down and left me in the Blake Street restaurant, on one knee, with the ring in hand.

Didn't even get the chance to finish the words, to ask for her hand and heart in marriage. She cut me off. "I can't do this," she said in a whisper and walked out.

I mustered up what focus I had left in me, ignored the Frank Sinatra music being piped through the PA system, paid our dinner bill, and left. My initial thought, go after her. Talk to her, plead with her, beg her to be with me; but why bother if she does not want to? I was torn up inside. I would be wasting my breath. Not quite sure how I spent three years with her and had no sign—no clue, not even an inkling—she no longer wanted this relationship.

I wished her mother would speak to me again, but I hadn't heard her voice during the three years we were together. She had gone silent.

Everything seemed so perfect between us, from our conversations, to sex, to our dreams and views on life. We had plans, shared visions, and always talked of our future. Now I was alone. In one fraction of a second, a single moment in time as they say. My heart felt heavy. I felt broken and lost.

I remembered a family story of a great uncle who got engaged once, then she called it off. He never dated again, never opened his heart to anyone, grew to be an old farmer and dairy producer spending his days alone, except with the livestock. At least he got to ask her. And she said yes, before changing her mind. He got to put the diamond of a promise on her finger, got to hear that one single word: "Yes." I didn't even get the proposal out.

Yet, something good did come from this. I discovered my soul had a price, and was worth selling.

Star Gazing

After leaving the restaurant, I set out on a drive to nowhere. The best thing for me at this time: a long drive. My mind was still bogged down with her rejection. Three years together, and now nothing but a wounded heart. Maybe more like a knife through my soul. "Christ," I mumbled under my breath, "I wished she would have died rather than shoot my proposal down."

I remember as a child when our beloved family dog, Dakota, died. My father took him to the vet, and I never saw him again. Never got to say goodbye. Never told what really happened. This felt the same. Rachael said, "I can't do this." *Can't do what,* I thought? *Can't marry me? Can't be with me? Why? What did I do? I guess I should at least be thankful she did not feed me the "it's-me-not-you" bullshit.*

"Shit," I cursed through my teeth and connected my fist to the dashboard. I think part of me hoped that the pain from the punch would take away the pain currently crushing my heart. It didn't. My emotions were racing and starting to get the best of me. I imagined her dying and her last breath being filled with apologies to me for breaking my dream of us. I also wondered what it would be like to actually take a life. *How do people murder and then go about their daily life, conducting everything as normal as putting on shoes?* Numerous horror movies came to mind, giving me a range of ideas. *I could tie her to a tree and leave her to the animals and the elements of nature. Burn her alive in bed as she sleeps. Inject her with a needle carrying the AIDS virus.*

Then a thought came to me. *Maybe I should pick up a girl and show her that she meant nothing to me; that I'm already over her and have moved on. We can flirt, laugh, and be affectionate in front of her. Kill her with jealousy. Make her regret turning down my proposal, have her beg me to take her back.*

A bit of fog rolled in from the nearby marsh, and I lost my bearings and became disoriented. Instead of heading home, where I would further wallow in my loss, I suddenly realized I was headed west along Durray Lane. I've lived in this area for five years and never ventured out here. Always told it was a lonely road that leads to nowhere. Sounds like a perfect place for me at the moment. Maybe a bit of fresh air and some stargazing would help clear my mind.

The road stretched on for about three miles. I could only see stonewalls and fields of overgrown weeds and grass. As the road narrowed, I pulled to the side and got out for some fresh air. Leaning back on my car, I gazed at the stars. A shooting star lit up the sky, and I wished for all my pain to go away. The knot in my stomach felt like someone gave me a solid punch, broke my heart into countless pieces, and left my soul crying. I remembered so much of her and our time together.

The ironic thing is, there was a time when she wanted to get married. She wanted the so-called

American dream: a large house, three kids, and the white picket fence. Not sure why, but I couldn't commit, not then, but I could now, and now she doesn't want that. Well, at least not with me.

Is there someone else? Could she be involved with another man, and that's why she turned me down? She often mentioned a guy Steve at work, how great he is, and how he's so helpful all the time. "He makes me laugh all day long," she shared with me. Maybe I should go to her place and see if I don't catch them in the act. The mere thought of another man being intimate with Rachael made me puke. After what felt like a cleaning out of my stomach and a dry heave, I wiped my mouth and looked about in the dark.

Through the moonlight, I noticed a footpath at the edge of the fence. I retrieved a flashlight from my trunk, thinking maybe a quick walk in nature would help clear my mind. In a short distance, it led up to a stonewall. Shining the light along it, I saw it needed a lot of repairs or to be rebuilt altogether. Many of the rocks were knocked off the wall, and thick weeds grew haphazard. For a moment, I stood still. I thought I heard music, but I knew more likely than not, my mind was playing tricks on me. I continued to follow the stonewall for about another ten minutes. Then I noticed a faint light, a glowing ember color. I turned off my flashlight and watched as this light moved about. I kept walking toward it when the stench of cigarettes hit me.

"Who goes there?" a voice asked in the darkness.

"A friendly stranger," I replied as I walked in the

direction of the voice.

"Not too often I hear 'friendly' and 'stranger' in the same sentence. What brings you out this way so late at night?"

Do I tell him? Do I share with this person how a woman I truly loved turned me down, broke my heart, and now I'm wandering through this open field, thinking of how I want her dead? Instead, I answer, "I'm just out clearing my mind."

"Very well," the old man said. At least, he sounded like an old man.

I tried to figure out why an old man was all alone out in an empty field late at night. After all, I knew why I was here, but why him? Maybe he had his heart shattered. Maybe he's a hermit.

"Well," he said.

"Excuse me?"

"Are you done?"

"Am I done with what?"

"Clearing your mind. That's what you said you were doing out here."

"I'm good," I said. "Mind if I ask why you're out here?"

"Sure, go ahead and ask," he said with a slight

laugh. "I'm reading the stars."

"Reading the stars?"

"That's what I said. By the way, the name's Jesse. Jesse Dean," he said as he extended out his hand.

I gripped his hand firmly. "Pleasure. I'm—"

Right then, a barking dog came darting across the field at us. I jumped back and got into a stance ready to ward off the vicious sounding beast of a dog.

"Come here, Dakota," Jesse said. "You're such a good girl." The dog ran a few circles around him.

"Your dog's name is Dakota?"

"Sure is."

"Wow. Same name as the dog I had as a child."

"I know."

"How could you have known that? We don't know each other, do we?"

"It's written in the stars," he said, looking up. "Truth is, my dog's name is Toby. I only said Dakota to show you the power of the stars if you know how to read them."

Even in the darkness, I could see Jesse's face, wrinkled and worn, as if he'd lived through a lot.

"You have a broken heart," he continued. "And now you're dealing with the emotions. You're questioning why, and you're probably filled with some doubt as to why you're here now, listening to an old man who claims to read the stars."

"Yes, I am. The broken heart just happened a couple of hours ago. Not sure why she turned me down and caused me to suffer like this."

"Because you gave her the opportunity," he said directly.

"I gave her the opportunity?"

"Of course, you did. You're human, after all."

"I'm afraid I'm not following."

Toby began to sniff around and found a spot to relieve herself. She then came up to me and rubbed against my leg. I gave her a few quick pets on the head, then looked at Jesse.

"Let me explain it like this. A bug, insect, or animal won't cause you to suffer unless it has a reason. You swat at a bee, you've irritated them, now it has a reason to make you suffer, so it stings you. Humans are different. We don't need a reason; we only need opportunity. So, you allowed her to cause you some suffering when you proposed. And by the looks of it, she did a bang-up job."

I gazed up at the vast sky, liquid black dotted with white specks, not a cloud to be seen. "You can tell all of that through the stars?"

"Sure can. See the partial moon?" he said, pointing up. "Follow it slightly north, and you'll see a very bright star amongst the others. This is known as your home star. It depicts males from females. Now, if you follow it east," he continued, as if drawing a line in the sky, "you'll see a small cluster of about five stars. This is the confusion you're experiencing right now. There's no direction."

"I don't mean to be—or come across as being—rude in saying this is all hooky, but what if I were someone else here tonight? You mean to tell me that the stars would have aligned up differently?"

"Well, no. The stars always align in the same patterns. They just read differently."

I looked at the stars, especially the cluster, and I could see what he meant by 'no direction,' and it's certainly how I felt.

"Have you ever read a book," he asked, "and thought, wow, what a great book? Then read it a second time and caught things you missed the first time? Or seen a movie for the second time and caught something different from the first time? That's what reading the stars is like. It reads differently every time."

He walked a few feet down a slope, turned, and looked back up at the sky. Toby followed him and then rested at his side. "Look over here." He again pointed to the sky. "See the Big Dipper? If you follow it to the end of its tail, then look south, three stars form a triangle. Everything in life is a triangle, and always one of the three points isn't good. Take a job, for instance. There are three things: work required, your boss, and rate of pay. One of the three isn't great."

A wind came through the field, and Toby perked up. Old man Jesse turned and looked along the stonewall. He held his hand out, palm facing up. Slowly, he turned and approached the center of the field. He brought his hands together and mumbled either a prayer or at least a few words. He then held his arms up to the sky, and a flash of lightning illuminated the field.

"Look over here," he said as if everything had gone back to business as usual. "Look across the field; see where the large tree stands? Follow it straight up to its highest branch. It looks like a star is set on top of it. That star is your spirit; it's sitting on top of the tree, for it is hurt. The two stars on either side are good and bad, or the yin and yang, or the angel and devil. There are also four stars just above it; they tell me you feel like you're trapped in a box. Like anyone or anything that is trapped, they want out."

"How do I get out?"

Jesse now looked at me. He took a step closer and put his hand on my shoulder. "That, my son, would be telling of the future, which the stars don't do. For that, you need to visit the crossroads."

"The crossroads?"

"Yes. At the crossroads, there will be a whisper, or what some call a ghost. It resides there, and its sole purpose is to whisper into your ear and try to interest you in whatever your fate may be." He pointed down the road. "Follow this road for exactly thirteen miles, and the crossroads will be Hallow Road and Graves Lane, beside the Old Soul River Cemetery. Stand at the center and listen for the whisper. It will be soft, but it will be clear."

"And that will tell me my future?"

"It will interest you in your fate, young man. But, be warned and take heed, don't venture out into the cemetery."

"Why not?"

"Evil has lurked in there for many years since the last burial. Trust me, don't go in there."

"Thank you, Jesse. I needed a bit of conversation."

"Woof, woof," Toby barked.

"And you too, Toby," I said, kneeling and rubbing her back.

I turned, took a few steps, and when I looked back, Jesse and Toby were gone.

The Crossroads
The headlights shone down the dirt road as my mind wandered to Rachael, to the conversation I had with

Jesse, to the crossroads. *What exactly am I to ask once I'm there? How does this work? I stand in the middle of the road and ask for advice? That must look pretty odd to any travelers passing by.*

Within fifteen minutes, the intersecting roads came into view. I came to a wooden post with two arrow signs, each pointing in opposite directions. I pulled to the side of the road and sat in my car for a moment, thinking about what I should ask.

"Speak your mind," a voice said.

"Excuse me? Who said that?"

"Come out to the crossroads and let me whisper in your ear."

"I'm not ready."

"Since you are here, you are ready."

I got out of my car and looked into the darkness, trying to see down each of the roads I did not travel. I then proceeded to walk into the center of the crossroads. *Not sure how this works.* I turned around as if expecting to see someone. Only the silence of the evening greeted me.

"Go on," a whisper of a voice said. "What is it you want? What is your true desire? Is it fame? Is it financial freedom? Perhaps you want true love like you thought you had with Rachael. Maybe you want something more?"

"I want to know why. Why did she dump me? Why did she say no even before I had a chance to ask for her hand in marriage? Why did she hurt me? What am I supposed to do now?"

"Go into the cemetery."

"The cemetery? Old man Jesse said not to."

The night became slightly colder. I glanced in the direction of the graveyard. Tombstones scattered about, a few tall monuments, the wrought iron gates attached to a stone archway entrance, and a stone wall surrounding the area, as if it were able to keep wandering spirits in. For some odd reason, it felt like it started beckoning me, although Jesse's voice rang in my ear not to go in there.

"You came here seeking guidance, did you not?"

"I did."

"Then go in the cemetery. It is from the dead we can guide you. We can find your true meaning, your so-called gift, or your 'why,' as you perhaps refer to it."

Again, I looked at the graveyard. My feet made crunching sounds as I walked toward the gates, pushed them ajar, and slipped through. It felt like my soul had become disturbed. Like it did not want to be there, perhaps trying to leave. Then I saw it. The glow in the middle of the cemetery. Two bright red dots. They didn't move, blink, or change color; they just appeared and stared at me.

I edged my way toward them and said, "Hello," with a shaky voice.

The red dots grew brighter.

A squirrel dashed by my feet, causing me to jump out of my skin. It ran up a tree and disappeared into the darkness.

"Come," said a whisper.

One step at a time, I made my way toward the two red dots.

"I've been waiting."

"Who are you?"

"What is it you desire?"

"I had the impression you would already know that."

"Very true, but you need to say it out loud; put it out there, so the spirits can hear you."

"Okay. I want to know why she turned me down."

Then, the two dots turned into a figure. The Devil and hell surrounded him. The cemetery briefly lit up in a hue of orange, and a fog rolled in across the ground as a flock of birds—bats maybe—took off into flight going in every direction. He looked through me with his fiery red eyes and drew in a breath, which sounded like a hiss. "Perhaps you want something that you can't achieve."

"What can't I achieve?" I asked, maybe not wanting to know the answer.

"How about murder?"

"Murder! You want me to murder someone? What on earth for?"

"I think it's murder you desire. Think about what it would feel like to snuff the life out of another human, particularly a certain someone who broke your heart."

"You want me to kill Rachael? She broke my heart, but that's no reason to kill her," I exclaimed.

"But, the thought is there nonetheless."

He was right. I had thought about her being dead. The old cliché of "if I can't have her, no one can." But I wouldn't follow through with anything like that. Rachael had always been sweet to me, fun to be with, and I still adored her. From the first night meeting her at the carnival to just hours ago, I remember all of our times together.

The moon turned to a shade of red. The Devil, with his staff in his hand, took a few steps backward. He faced the open cemetery and reminded me, "We all end up here. We all complete the other side of the dash, some just sooner than others."

The wind picked up, going from a breeze to a brisk,

steady offshore gale. The trees bent, branches were stripped of their leaves, and not a creature, other than the Devil and myself, moved about the graveyard.

He continued, "Don't be frightened of murder; we're all capable. Every one of your kind has had the thought. Some people wish it on others; some even plan it, and then there are the people who follow through. And some of those people blame me." He turned around to face me. "As if it were I who pulled the trigger, or had thrust the cold steel blade of a knife into another's heart. How primitive of your kind."

"Primitive?"

"I would not kill someone with a gun or a butcher's utensil. I would kill them through fear."

"How?"

God vs. Focalor

The Devil perched himself on a gravestone and rested his staff on the ground. He waved his hand over his head, and clouds came from nowhere, blocking the moon. "On a night just like this," he said, his voice even raspier. "I, a gentleman back then, broad, strong, handsome, had worked to earn enough money to purchase my freedom. As a known indentured servant, I had to pay double because I didn't believe God. And before you start to throw all of your memorized Bible verses at me, let me tell you this: I've been to Heaven, and it's not real. There is no glorious life after your last breath travels away; there is no Hallelujah; no angels and harps; no souls or spirits frolicking from your life on earth."

"Well, what is Heaven then? What happens when we die?"

The Devil raised his arm over the ground, and his staff shot up into his hand. He glided off the tombstone and stood inches from my face. His breath smelled stale, and my heart raced. "Let me tell you what Heaven is. It's void. It's a tunnel of white noise. Do you know who's in Heaven? Do you?" he hollered, stabbing his staff into the ground.

Thunder clamored above, lightning rolled through the sky, and the cemetery fell silent. He pulled his staff from the ground and pointed it an inch from my forehead. I could feel the heat coming off the tip. His staff reached down into hell and had collected some brimstone.

"N-n-no, I don't," I said, with my eyes closed and body shaking.

The Devil lowered his staff, and I let out a sigh of relief and opened my eyes. He made a quick turn, causing his cape to swirl. "Heaven is full of a breed you never heard of. A race you humans refer to as 'others,' who don't conform to your belief that defies all the laws of nature and the universe. They were banned from the earth by your so-called Almighty. What your little prayer book doesn't tell you is about the battle that raged between God and Focalor, known as the Great Duke of Hell."

"Are you saying God was once evil?"

"Your God was once human," he answered. "He was once like you; I was once like you. We felt pain, joy, sadness, and excitement, but then something larger than us both thought it would be a good idea to separate the elements; to divide eternity into good and bad. What you now call Heaven and Hell. That's when good and evil, as you've come to understand it, were born. Before that, everything equaled harmony. The Division! It sparked the great separation of everything. The catalyst of night versus day, dark versus light, and God versus Focalor."

More thunder rolled across the sky, and the wind grew to a steady breeze. All I could see were his red eyes and the tip of his staff, glowing in a shade of lucent yellow. For a moment, I had an odd feeling, like the world had stilled and time had stopped. Oh, how I hoped this horrible nightmare, or alcohol-induced, mind-racing, crazy story, would end, but when a loud clap of thunder echoed throughout the cemetery and rattled my bones, he stood there, towering over me. A vision from Sandman, this was not. I was awake, coherent, and terrified.

"God wanted it all," he continued. "All the seven sins you try to refrain from—he was greed, lust, gluttony, sloth, wrath, envy, and pride, all rolled into one. I find it rather amusing how your Good Book defines those as sins as if saying, 'These are all the fun things, yet you must avoid them at all costs.' I sometimes question if you humans were put on earth to live in pleasure or live in a vacuum, where everything you do comes down to judgment. Do you or do you not get to go through pearly gates? You've been living a lie. You've been living with this great big hope, this so-called promise, but I'm here to tell you that your Good Book is perhaps the best fairy tale ever written. I lived once as you do, and I know what happened between God and Focalor. They battled for three straight days, with no mercy between them.

"Focalor had been banished to the soil below, while God had all the peace of the clouds. Focalor challenged this, and God accepted. The more generous soul, the universe, would decide on the outcome of this challenge. God and Focalor met at midnight, beside Bethany's hillside, where your Mother Mary resided as a child. God showed no fear, and Focalor no remorse.

"When the moon rose directly above, their challenge began. One hundred men gathered atop the hill and later scribed into their books the details of what they witnessed. And what they witnessed had never been translated into your Holy Book. Since the beginning of time, you've only been told what the greater entities want you to know. This is the truth," he said, as he waved his arm to the sky. The clouds parted, and the moonlight shone down on us.

"God had superior strength. He grabbed Focalor by the throat, pinned him down, and made his threat known. He squeezed hard, clenched his fingers tight, and told Focalor he would never share eternity with him. With that, God lifted Focalor off the ground and hurled him into the side of the hill. Focalor rose to his feet and let out a howl, as if he were summoning an animal—or signaling a spirit for strength. He lunged at God, knocking him back into a small tree. The tree gave way, and when Focalor picked up the solid branch, it turned into a staff. He pointed it at God and said, 'I will rule all three kingdoms—heaven, hell, and earth.' With that, he stabbed the staff at God, who rolled to his side, letting the staff sink three feet into the soil.

"Focalor, now furious, turned around as God hit him in the chest and sent him back twelve feet. Focalor stood up, and God stood right there, in his face. Focalor spat at him and gave him an uppercut to his stomach. God hurled over and fell to his knees. Focalor grabbed him by the chin and lifted him to his feet. 'Eternity will be all mine,' he hollered as he threw God back to the ground. A loud thud echoed to the top of the hillside.

"God quickly spun around, sweeping Focalor at his feet, knocking him to the earth. He then rolled on top of Focalor and said, 'The soil under the earth will be your only Kingdom.' Then God brought about rage so violent, so immense, so uncontrollable. Focalor focused his energy on retrieving his staff, still three feet into the earth.

"God's fury continued. Focalor's staff began vibrating as he stretched out his arm and hand. As the staff shot free from the ground, God intercepted it, broke it in two, and stabbed Focalor with the two pieces.

"He pierced his heart and then his soul. Focalor lay motionless in a pool of his blood. God stood above him and said, 'Heaven and Earth are mine. The inferno of Hell is now your home for the next one thousand years.' With that, Focalor vanished into the ground below, letting out a mighty scream heard throughout the land."

"Why has none of this ever made it into the Bible?"

"Because your God, your Almighty, did not want his followers to know that truth—that he, once a demon himself, had been on the path to control the universe. And he lied."

"God lied?"

"Indeed! He promised Focalor his tour in Hell would be one thousand years. We are still living out eternity. He furthered promised the sea and wind, and full range of what he could do with each. Hurricanes, tornadoes, tsunamis, and the rage and hell that can go with all of them. But then God gave all of that to Mother Nature."

As dawn began to break, I could see his bright red eyes start to dim against the sunlight. He pulled his hood over his head and leaned heavily on his staff. "I can make you an offer, a mighty sweet offer. I will kill Rachael, and in return, you give me your soul."

I froze. So much of me wanted her to suffer, to feel my pain, my heartache, and how I now doubt myself; the "what's-wrong-with-me?" kind of thinking.

"Her death will set all of your pain free. No more thoughts of her, no more torture to your heart, you'll be free, just as you wish."

"What am I going to do with no soul?"

"My dear friend," the Devil said, putting his arm around me and pulling me close. "Imagine a life with no pain. No more heartache. After all, I remind you, it's what you wished for."

I hesitated for a moment. I couldn't imagine Rachael dead. But the pain gnawing at me grew to be unbearable. "Let's do it," I said, surprising myself.

"Splendid. I will see upon her death, then rendezvous with you following her demise."

Before I could utter another word or ask another question, and more importantly, change my mind, he vanished.

***

I stopped at the hospital to visit Rachael. She lay there with tubes coming out of her nose and needles sticking into her arm. A small smile grew across her lips when I walked in with flowers and a teddy bear.

"Aren't you the guy from the carnival three years ago?" she said in a soft voice followed with a slight laugh. She loved to refer to me as "the guy from the carnival."

I smiled at her. "That would be me, but you shouldn't be talking. You should be resting." As I put her flowers on the counter, I noticed her chart. Scanning it, I noticed the box checked in the upper right. It stated *patient stage four*, with a note, *three days*. I knew instantly it meant three days to live.

I gave her the teddy bear and tried to be upbeat.

"I'm so sorry," she whispered. "I was just scared. When I get better, I will marry you—that is if you still want me."

"Please, Rachael. Save your strength. Don't talk."

She squeezed the teddy bear, and I thought of how badly I wanted her. I wanted her to kick this stage four cancer and marry me. As I thought this, I could feel a heat surge through me. The same heat I felt when the Devil held his staff to my forehead.

I needed to get back to the cemetery and tell the Devil the deal is off. He must let her recover fully, so I can be with her.

"A deal is a deal," said a voice. I glanced over at Rachael, who had fallen into a deep sleep.

"I don't want her to die," I said.

"A deal is a deal, my friend. Her death for your soul."

"Look—"

"I said we will rendezvous after her demise."

A Promise Is a Promise

I stood at her gravesite, and the words from the minister offering her soul to heaven fell silent upon my ears. I watched the pallbearers lower her into her eternal resting place. Through my veins raced a mixture of feelings from emptiness, to being numb, to shallow. As if I had no heart, no spirit, no—

"Soul," whispered the wind.

I didn't go to her parents' place for the after gathering. It would only be more tears and "I'm sorry's" filling the room. Instead, I traveled back to the crossroads to meet with the Devil.

***

Just as eerie in the daylight as in the evening, the cemetery still had a forbidding atmosphere. I made my way out to the center and looked about the grounds. "Where are you?" I hollered. The wind responded with a breeze, stirring some leaves, and spooked a mouse who dashed across one of the stones. "Are you here?" Again, a slight flurry of wind.

I turned to face the crossroads and wondered why I had not heeded the old man's advice of "don't venture into the cemetery." The Devil's presence floated beside me. I could feel the stabbing of his eyes that stared for too long. Looking across to the back end of the cemetery, there he was. Fully dressed in black, with his staff in his hand, he approached me.

As he got closer, I could see his face lined with wrinkles, a small wart dotted his nose, and his eyes were solid black, like ink. His breathing turned heavy and had a grim tone to it, almost like a wheeze. "You are early, I see. Ready to make good on your promise?" he asked in his raspy voice.

"I told you, I changed my mind. I didn't want her to die."

"A promise is a promise."

With one swift motion, he shot his staff into the ground and took a step closer. "You can't break or renegotiate your promise with me. Our deal has not changed; your soul for the death of Rachael. Remember, the girl who broke your heart into a million pieces? Why, even you said, 'I wished she would have died rather than shoot my proposal down.' And here I deliver on that desire, only for you to throw it back at me. And why? Because she changed her mind? Because you have this false notion and belief that marrying her would be your forever happiness? How foolish. It's time for you to keep your end of the promise and pay now."

He flipped his hood back off his head. His ears were droopy, full of hair, and one had an earring of a pentagram. His bald head looked like a road map of veins, but instead of blue and red, they were black. With his long, frail finger, he pointed at me, almost touching my nose, and said in a hoarse, phlegm-filled, hushed tone, "Time to feed my hunger."

Other spirits came up through the ground and surrounded me. Noticing there were close to thirty of them, I realized this Devil was Focalor. I was about to have my soul ripped from me by the Great Duke of Hell himself. I let out a scream that traveled unheard as they wrestled me to the ground and waited for a command from Focalor.

He knelt beside me, and in his hoarse whisper, said, "You are now the ghost of the crossroads." Focalor then shot his hand down my throat. I twisted and turned as the legion of spirits held me down. I could feel all my energy leaving my body as he tore my soul from my insides.

I let out a cough, and the legions released their grip. I rolled over onto my side, puked, and spit out a bit of blood. "What happens to me now that I have no soul, you Bastard?"

"You will reside at the crossroads and interest travelers in their fate," he said.

A bright light, a sudden flash, then my soul enveloped into his body. Focalor turned from an old, haggard man into a young man, into a young soul. The legions disappeared back into the ground, and I slowly raised myself off the ground.

I felt empty inside, like hunger pangs but couldn't eat. My soul was now gone. Focalor gone. I sat unnoticed on the edge of the crossroads.

Crossroads Part II

One early morning, just after midnight, I heard a car engine hum in the near distance. A van rolled into the crossroads, and a young woman got out. She looked about the area, noting the cemetery. I could tell a slight chill shot through her. She walked out to the center of the intersection.

"Well, I'm here," she said in a low voice. "Old man Jesse sent me."

I walked up to her, keeping her unaware of my presence. "I can guide you," I whispered.

"Who said that?" she asked, snapping her head left and right. "Who's here?"

"You've come to the crossroads, and it is I who will interest you in your fate."

She turned around and looked down both roads, then cautiously followed my voice into the cemetery.

A Failed Clown

Introduction: This piece came about when my flight from Dallas to Fort Myers was canceled due to tornado warnings. In my hotel room, I suggested to my Facebook friends to post some writing prompts. I'd pick the winner and write a short story, which the winner got to read before anyone else. This wasn't the winner, but it stuck with me. The prompt was, "After I failed clown school..."

It happened because Samuel had failed clown school. His dream of joining the circus had been crushed, if not totally out of his grasp. Depression set in, and he tried to drown his wallowing through a fifth of Jack Daniels every night.

A year later, he found himself perched on the bridge with a view of jagged rocks below. To him, they were hollering, "Jump now!"

In a drunken stupor, he shuffled his feet closer to the edge. The gusty wind blew his greasy hair into his bearded face. Samuel glanced down, then looked straight ahead. The beauty of the mountains, covered with pine trees and a lone eagle in the middle of its soar was not enough to get him to step back and down off the bridge to safety.

Just one more step, he thought.

He closed his eyes and was instantly taken back to a time of being dressed in his polka-dotted outfit, big round red nose, size 16 shoes, and a wig of rainbow-colored hair; doing what he loved, performing at a kid's birthday party doing magic tricks, and sharing funny jokes with the crowd of ten-year-olds and adults alike. After making some balloon animals and giving the birthday boy a jovial birthday cheer from Sammy the Silly Clown, his life changed.

At that moment, he reflected on how his life was nothing. He had no family, no children, no spouse, and no real friends. He realized his life was almost like a mirage. Like he existed, but who cared? Would anyone miss him if he were gone?

When Samuel arrived home after the party, he checked his mail, looked down the street to the left, then right, as was his routine, then proceeded down his walkway to the front door. He climbed out of his outfit, washed the make-up from his tired face, and sat in his recliner.

Shuffling through his mail, there it was. An official notice from the Circus Center Clown School University. Hope surged through him. Could it be that his life's pursuit was about to become a reality? Samuel tore it open, tossing the envelope to the floor. He unfolded the letter which was housed inside, read the words … and began to cry.

The letter informed him he did not pass clown school because he did not meet all the criteria. He had missed too many days. This would be the first night Samuel started drinking, followed by another bender the next night, and so on. This would become his routine, until a year later, when he decided jumping off the bridge would be better. Ending his life would be the answer to his growing depression.

He released his grip from the cable and steadied himself against the wind. Drawing in a deep breath, he released it slowly. He pivoted carefully toward the road and looked left, then to the right. Then he jumped from the ledge letting out a slight laugh as he landed on the sidewalk.

Thank God the booze wore off in time once again, he thought. He peered over the railing. "That's a mighty long way down, and I don't know how to fly," he said out loud with no one to hear.

Samuel walked home after being on the bridge, which had also become his routine. He climbed into bed to sleep off the rest of the alcohol.

***

His routine changed the following morning when he didn't wake up. It would be another month before his landlord discovered his decaying body after neighbors reported a strange, foul order emanating from Samuel's house.

Sammy the Silly Clown was buried in a pauper's

grave, in the far west corner section of the town's cemetery, wearing his outfit and make-up. He never knew that following his death, the circuses all came to a close, just the way vaudeville gave way to the cinema.

In his mind, Samuel would have thought it was just routine; after all, isn't there a failed clown in all of us?

The Tomb Sprinkled with Blood

Introduction: JWC Publishing held a horror writing class in October 2017. We learned about the elements to make a great horror story, how to pace your storytelling, and had award-winning horror writer Michael Hebler as a special guest. Each student had to write a short horror story that we privately published in an anthology titled The Humanity of Fear. *This was my contribution.*

The Windless Hallow Cemetery sat on the hill in the far section of town. Abandoned back in the 1950s, when the Chancers Funeral Home acquired property across town for a new burial ground, and began burials there shortly after the train wreck of 1952.

Growing up, I heard the tall tale of a wandering spirit who roamed the old Windless Hallow graveyard at five past midnight. It, or he or she, would pace up and down, back and forth through the rows of headstones, then stop always at the marker that bared no name. The only grave in the yard not accounted for. Rumor told the story of a stranger discovered one morning hanging from a tree and never identified. The odd thing about this marker, it was sprinkled with blood. If this wandering spirit was buried in the unnamed grave, the blood would make sense with the superstitious folklore that says, "To raise them, sprinkle the tomb with blood and call them by name."

Yet, no one knew his name. Or where he came from and why he hung from a tree along the dirt road, which lead to Benton's Farm.

Morton Willoughby, out for his usual early morning stroll thirty years ago, with his cane in one hand, and a fine Cuban cigar in the other, noticed a man leaning against a tree. Only when he got closer did he realize the man was not leaning but hanging about six inches from the ground.

His face was pasty white, and rigor mortis had set in. Morton ran to Benton's Farm and called the authorities. Seven minutes later, the dirt road had two police cars racing with sirens screaming, one fire truck, and an ambulance.

The stranger was taken down and hauled away to the morgue. A search through his clothing and an autopsy revealed no clues to his identity. His official cause of death: "broken neck from hanging." He was buried in the Windless Hallow Cemetery without a service. Four days after the burial, a stone appeared, but no engraving on it other than R.I.P. and the date of May 9, 1953.

Morton seems to have been the only person in town to visit this gravesite regularly. He'd spend a few hours every Sunday following church, sitting in front of the stone and staring at it. On a few occasions, he had his Bible and read a few passages. He did this until his death in 1964.

I can't explain why I'm now the one to spend Sunday mid-afternoons here, sitting where Morton sat, staring at this stone. There is no connection; I feel no energy like a spirit is around me while I'm here. Never has there been a story in my family that we may be related to this stranger, so I can't begin to fathom why I'm so drawn to be here.

The Windless Hallow Cemetery was officiated in 1885, and since then has interned more than six hundred souls, none of which have any relationship to me. The first to be buried here was Benjamin Atwater, a blacksmith who succumbed to smallpox. He proclaimed a curse had been set upon him on his death bed, and the townspeople would suffer dearly when the hanged man returned.

The townspeople and the local paper played this down. To them, it was merely the side effects of the disease. Oddly enough, this cemetery became non-active after the burial of the hanged man. By now, the locals had forgotten the warning given by Atwater more than 130 years ago.

Then one Sunday afternoon, I didn't go. I didn't feel the calling or the pull or the need or desire that I should. That particular Sunday, I settled on my couch and fell asleep. I awoke at 11:45 in the evening after hearing a voice whisper, "Come visit me."

I rubbed my eyes, shook my head, and through the dark, made my way to the bathroom. After splashing some cold water on my face and feeling more awake, I could see in the mirror the reflection of a figure standing behind me. I quickly turned around, and it was gone.

Turning back to the mirror, it somehow had steamed up and written on the fogged mirror was, "Come visit me."

I splashed more water on my face and wiped the mirror clean of the message. Going from room to room throughout my apartment, I searched for the figure I had seen, but there was no trace of anyone being in my home but me.

The next thing I can remember is being in my car, driving to the cemetery. I pulled through the stone archway and traveled slowly up the hill to the far end of the graveyard. Passing monuments, headstones, potted flowers, flags, all of which appeared spooky in the dark as my headlights cast oblong shadows against each object. At least fifty feet from the other lots in the corner of the yard, I saw the unnamed grave. As I stood in front of the stone, an eerie feeling crept through me. It felt like a patch of cold air sliced right through my clothes into my body. I shivered for a moment.

"Why am I here?" I asked no one or perhaps asked the stone.

A cloud passed, covering the moon, and the graveyard enveloped into darkness, like being in a sea of black liquid.

"I need to tell you what happened," a voice said.

"Who said that?" I hollered into the darkness.

Silence. A creepy, deafening silence. My heart stopped, and my mind couldn't keep up with the crazy scenarios I started creating. I looked around but could see nothing in the darkness. "Is anybody here?"

"Yes. I am."

"Who are you?"

"I'm who you refer to as the spiritual wanderer. I am who the newspapers described as the unknown soul, the one buried all alone with not as much as a reading from our Good Book."

I could feel the wind pick up as he spoke. However, this wind had a certain chill to it, like walking inside a freezer after being out in the hot sun. "What do you want with me?" I hoped he wouldn't answer.

"Revenge."

"For what?"

"It's quite simple," the voice said. The blood sprinkled on the tomb began to illuminate. In the distance, a dog, maybe a wolf let out a howl, and I could now see this ghost—tall with piercing red eyes, and strips of cloth hanging from his shoulders. "I need you to lure my killer here so I can seek my revenge."

"But no one knows who you are, and the killer was never found. It's a cold case."

"I will tell you who, and you will bring him to me."

"But I would need evidence, and the police will have to be involved. They would have to reopen the case. I can't do all of that. I can't go to the authorities and say I know who hung that man sixty years ago because the dead man's ghost told me so. They'll lock me up for being crazy. And, it's been sixty years ... is your killer even alive?"

"Don't concern yourself with the police. Just follow my instructions."

The blackness of night dissipated slightly. The spirit sat upon his marker.

"I'm sorry, but I can't do it, I just can't. I'm not going to lure some old man here for you to seek revenge on him."

"Oh, but you will. See the blood sprinkled on this tomb?" he asked, jumping down and stepping aside.

I nodded.

"It's yours," he said in his raspy, scratchy voice.

"Mine?"

"It's the folklore coming true," he said. "I've sprinkled the tomb with your blood and called you by name."

"Are you saying I'm dead?"

"For a long time. You died of smallpox, and your name is Atwater. Benjamin Atwater."

"The curse," I whispered under my breath.

"That's right," the ghost said. "The curse in which you warned the townspeople to heed fell on deaf ears. But you can stop this curse by bringing to me the man who hung me. Let me have my revenge, and I'll dispel the curse, and you, you can then rest in peace."

I thought for a moment. "Then I can rest in peace? You mean, I'm the one who wandered of this graveyard? I thought it was you?"

He stood there, not saying a word, as if he wanted me to figure it out. The sun started to break above the entrance to the graveyard. The blackness of night had soaked into the ground.

"If I'm Benjamin Atwater, and you're the hanged man, then who was Morton Willoughby, and why did he visit this grave every Sunday?"

"Ah, good ol' Mort Willy. He was twelve years old when you died in 1885 but strongly believed in the curse you had forewarned the townspeople about. Enough so that he dedicated his Sunday afternoons to being here, with your soul, and trying to contact you in hopes of preventing the curse from coming. But he was also here for another reason."

The wind picked up and rustled a few leaves. The trees swayed, and their branches made knocking sounds as they brushed up against one another.

"What's the other reason?"

"His son is my killer."

"Jonathan Willoughby? Old man JW killed you? I can hardly believe that," I exclaimed. "He has to be one of the most respected people in town. He's a former fireman and former mayor. He's like the grandfather of the town and acts as the town historian."

"And by having held the position of mayor, and now as town historian, he has been able to keep his horrible deed covered up in many layers. Morton sat out here every Sunday, also praying for forgiveness for his son's actions. The only thing is I don't forgive. So, you need to bring Jonathan to me, and in return, I'll stop the curse."

"What exactly is the curse?"

"The curse would unleash a hell never witnessed by humankind before. It would bring about rage, fury, and a level of madness no military power has ever faced. If you imagine the most brutal pain you've ever experienced, the curse will make that seem like a pleasant day at the beach."

"Why is the curse to strike here? What happened to cause this?"

The ghost looked around the graveyard. "See that group of stones?" he pointed to a cluster of headstones that faced the fence near a line of trees. "That's the Trotten family. Prior to the war of the colonies against the King, they were banished from their mother country of England and forced to reside here in Beacon Mills. Among them was Ezekiel Trotten, a self-proclaimed worshiper of Satan. He brought the devil to this town, who took a stand against Christianity and all those who believed in the Good Book. It was Morton Willoughby's family, a long line of preachers, who fought with him until Morton's great-grandfather killed Ezekiel's son."

The ghost hung his head down. "I was his son, Thaddaeus Trotten. And I have died many times over. Jonathan Willoughby felt convicted in his actions of hanging me because he knew my family heritage and feared for the town that I'd bring the devil back. I promise you, I'm not the devil, but for me to be set free, I must take revenge, and you must help me."

"Why me?"

"Because you're Benjamin Atwater. You awoke the curse and poked the sleeping devil."

I stood there frozen. The sun rose steadily over the line of trees, and the ghost became harder to see. I did not know any of this about my family. Never was I told of our family lineage and the dark skeletons hiding in our closet. Taking a deep breath, I exhaled slowly and felt tired.

"You must go now. Go and bring Jonathan here, to

this stone, so that I may seek revenge, and so you can rest in peace."

I squinted my eyes as I glanced into the sun, and he disappeared.

As I began to walk toward the gate, I realized I was dead. That I was a ghost or a spirit maybe trapped between reality and the afterlife. In my heart, I wanted to rest in peace, so I decided to find JW and bring him here.

***

The following morning, I visited the Beacon Mills Historical Society. There, sitting at an old post office style roll-top desk, was JW. I glided around the room and looked over his shoulder. He was busy shuffling through some newspaper clippings about the hanged man—Thaddaeus Trotten. Perhaps it's his way of expressing remorse, reading and reliving the events and feeling guilty. Or he may have been patting himself on the back, as if it were a victory to this deed that he thought he saved the town from.

I let out a deep exhale and scattered the clippings about the table and floor. "Oh, my," Jonathan said as he bent down and started to collect them.

I then slammed the door shut, causing him to stop in mid bend and look in my direction. He walked over to the door and studied it before slowly opening it and looking down the hallway. "Hello?" he shouted, although his voice was weak. "Anybody here?"

Next, I turned the lights off, then back on. "What in Sam Hill?" He grabbed his coat, but before he could make it to the door, I took a book down from the shelves, which to Jonathan looked like it was floating, placed it on the table, and opened to a page about the history of the hanged man.

"Who's doing this?"

I tugged on the window shade, letting it retract back up, making a loud *clack-clack-clack* sound. Jonathan jumped, nearly out of his skin, and looked at the window as the shade came to a stop.

"This is not funny, not at my age. You could give me a heart attack. Do you want that on your conscience?"

I glided over to the dry erase board and, with a green marker, wrote "Windless Hallow Cemetery."

Jonathan stood watching. "Well, what about it?"

"Go there tonight. Midnight," I wrote.

"What on earth for?"

Without responding, I left and slammed the door.

***

At ten till midnight, I began to pace about the graveyard, awaiting Jonathan's arrival. With one minute to go, he showed up, shuffling along with his cane.

"Well, I'm here," he said. "What is it you want with me?"

I appeared so he could see me. "The hanged man will be here shortly. He needs to seek his revenge before a curse befalls Beacon Mills."

"Curse?"

"Yes."

"I don't know anything about a curse. Did you drag me out here during the witching hour, thinking I could dispel some phony old tall tale?"

Right then, the hanged man, the son of Ezekiel Trotten, appeared.

Jonathan took a step back and gasped.

"Remember me?" Thaddaeus asked. "Remember the day you invited me out for a cup of coffee, then you had this need to show me something at Benton's Farm, and along the way, you hit me in the head from behind like a coward. Then strung me up in a tree. Do you recall that day, Willoughby? Do you?!" he shouted with his voice echoing through the graveyard.

Jonathan began to whimper.

"I hung there for three days before your father, of all people, discovered me. Now, I must seek my revenge on you."

"I-I-I had to it," Jonathan spit out.

"You had to?" Thaddaeus questioned.

"Yes."

Right then, a patch of fog materialized from the ground and sprang upward. It swirled and formed into another spirit.

"I told him to do so, without question," the spirit said.

"Well, I see ol' Mort Willoughby is here to rescue his son. How charming," Thaddaeus mocked.

"I'm the one you need to seek revenge on."

"Very well, then."

Morton and Thaddaeus began to circle each other. Within a second, they were entangled and choking one another. Morton gave a mighty shove and sent Thaddaeus flying into a tomb. Thaddeus scrambled to his feet and moved toward Morton. With one hand, he lifted Morton off the ground and threw him into some low hanging tree branches near the Trotten section of the graveyard.

"Benjamin!" Thaddaeus hollered. "Kill Jonathan now if you ever want to rest in peace."

I looked over to Jonathan as he began to run as best he could at his feeble age. Picking up a rock, I smashed the back of his head, and he fell. His blood sprinkled the tomb with no name engraved upon it.

"Jon!" Morton screamed. "No!"

"Begone!" Thaddaeus demanded, and Morton swirled back into a mass of fog, then soaked back into the ground. Then he turned to me. "You can now rest in peace."

"What happens next? I rest in peace for all eternity?"

"Yes."

Thaddaeus disappeared into the night.

***

"Daddy," eight-year-old Caleb said. "Who's buried here?"

"Well, I'm not sure, son. There's no name on the stone."

"But someone is buried there?"

"Oh, for sure there is. When I was your age, my father, your granddad, told me all about the hanged man buried here. Perhaps that is who is there."

"And what are these spots?" Caleb asked, pointing to the unnamed gravestone.

"It's part of a superstition."

"A super what?"

"A superstition. It's where people tend to believe something that's perhaps not real."

Caleb touched the stone, rubbing his fingers along the rough edges. "What's the superstition for this, Daddy?"

"It says if you want to contact who's buried there, sprinkle some blood and call them by name."

"I want to meet my great-great granddad."

Caleb's father let out a slight laugh. "Go ahead. His name was Jonathan Willoughby."

Caleb stared at the gravestone and shouted, "Jonathan Willoughby!"

They both stood still for a moment.

"I guess he's not home," Caleb said.

"I guess not, little buddy. Let's get going; mom is waiting for us."

As they walked away, a small tremor vibrated through the yard, and Caleb heard a faint voice: "Come visit me."

Final Words

Well my friend, you've read some very eclectic stories! I trust you've enjoyed each one. Perhaps you've read the book in one sitting. Maybe you read a story each night before going to bed. No matter your reading preference, I hope I've obtained my goal of providing you with enjoyment.

I'm sure I'll write another collection of stories. Until then, feel free to share this book with your friends and family; it's always good to share something enjoyable!

All the Best,
T.M. Jacobs

Acknowledgments

No book is done by oneself. It's a team effort from the writer, editor, proofreader, beta-readers, to critiquers. I'm thankful for all the feedback on these stories from the Sarasota Creative Writers Meetup, the Florida's Writers Association Nokomis Chapter, and Fire Writers.

Simon Presland, for his editorial skills and enthusiasm on this project.

Michael Attebery, for his keen eye on the proofread.

Kathleen, my mirror in life, business partner, travel companion, and best friend!

Always, Mom and Dad, for their encouragement for me to always pursue my dreams of writing.

About the Author

T.M. Jacobs, a native to the shoreline area of Connecticut, now resides in various locations along the east coast with his wife (an award-winning writer, children's book author and founder of Northern Dawn Awards) traveling and working from their RV motorhome. He has published 14 books (one of which was featured on C-SPAN), over 400 articles published in various newspapers and magazines, teaches classes on writing and publishing, and is currently the owner of JWC Publishing. He is the founder and former editor for Patriots of the American Revolution magazine and has been a freelance writer for over 35 years.

LinkedIn: https://www.linkedin.com/in/timjacobsghostwriter/
Facebook: www.facebook.com/JacobsWritingConsultantsLlc/
Twitter: @Jacobs1776Tim
Website: www.jacobswc.com
Email: tjacobs@jacobswc.com